IAN BILLINGS

Ian Billings is a writer, poet, stand-up comic, actor and hiccuper. He was born about a year before his first birthday and is now taller than he was then. He tours the world performing stand-up comedy for kids in schools, libraries and arts centre. So far he has been funny in Germany, Cyprus, Egypt, Australia, Qatar, Russia, Thailand, Vietnam, Jordan, the Moon, United Arabs Emirates and Malaysia. – one of these is untrue. His books include "Sam Hawkins, Pirate Detective" and "Space Rocks!" which became an app for iPhones and iPads and can be heard on British Airways Flights. He has an MA from the University of Birmingham and is looking forward to collecting a few more letters soon.

Ian loves writing about himself in the third person – in fact, he's doing it right now – and says the secret to good writing is first putting the vowels in place, padding it out with a few consonants then scattering some punctuation marks here and there.

If you want to look at him go to www.ianbillings.com - if you don't, go somewhere else.

Move along now. Nothing more to read here.

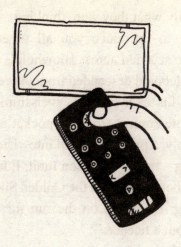

Chapter One
ST SMUGG'S
VERY PRIVATE SCHOOL

"Friends, welcome to my domain!"

The voice belonged to Oleg Blowhole and he was an extremely naughty boy – head boy of St Smugg's Very Private School and one of the most villainous criminals ever to twang a catapult. He stood proudly at the top of a huge shining white table, which dominated the huge pristine white office, and ran his hand through his slick black hair. He flicked on a glimmering light and struck a few poses he'd seen in a clothing catalogue. "You're probably wondering why I sent for you."

The five visitors around the table exchanged glances.

That was exactly what they were thinking.

"Allow me to introduce you all to each other." A slithering smile scurried across Blowhole's face as a large interactive whiteboard descended from the ceiling narrowly missing Snot, his ever-present, ever-stupid servant. He slipped a remote control from his pocket and zapped the screen. Suddenly, a picture popped into vision.

"Chu Chong – third generation Inuit. Educated at Igloo Preparatory School. Received the Golden Snowball for Ice-Cream Making. Currently on the run for selling chewy penguins without a licence."

The screen flashed to another picture.

"Eva Gabriella Chomp – uneducated, heritage unknown. Parents believed to be very big in the world of underpants. Self-taught lollipop manufacturer. Currently sought by Bolivian authorities for the Infamous Gobstopper Swindle."

The picture changed once more.

"Hank J Twizzler the Third. Born both New Jersey and New Hampshire for tax reasons. Inherited three million dollar bubble gum industry from Hank J Twizzler the First. Currently on the run from Hank J Twizzler the Second. Convicted of possessing fraudulent gum stickers."

Again the picture changed.

"Viscount Herbert Dibdab, last of a generation of British sweetie makers. Descended from Lord Horatio Dibdab who sold gobstoppers as cannonballs at the Battle of Waterloo. Disgraced the family name by supplying out-of-date candyfloss at the Eton Scoffing Race. Currently under surveillance by New Scotland Yard for his dodgy toffee trafficking activities and finally…"

The picture changed once more.

"Flip Wrigley, born in a pet shop in New South Wales, brought up on a diet of rabbit food and chives. Sworn hatred of vegetables ever since. Active in Rights for Candy and League Against Healthy Fruit. Under investigation by the Sydney Police Department for smearing chocolate spread on innocent radishes throughout Australia."

The whiteboard clicked off as Blowhole finished. All five visitors shifted uncomfortably at the thought of being tumbled and their schemes uncovered. But what could they do? All five decided to keep their cool. But Blowhole was far from finished.

"So what do you all have in common?"

Snot, Blowhole's ever-present ever-stupid servant, held up his hand to answer the question.

"Not you!" sighed Blowhole, and Snot slunk over to the biscuit tray.

No one answered the question. Blowhole asked it again and no one answered it again.

Snot put up his hand.

"Oh, alright, you!"

"What they all have in common, sir, is they are all deeply involved in the confectionery industry and all have reason to conceal their naughty goings-on. And you, Mr Blowhole, have evidence to put them behind bars for years." A proud grin tore across Snot's face like a rip in a bed sheet.

"Very good, Snot, you may dunk a biscuit!"

Snot dunked.

"Indeed, and that is why you are all going to help me. You have no choice! I have an ingenious plan which will throw the world of candy into turmoil. You are the finest candy barons on earth and you are going to help me in the greatest sweetie scam in the history of the planet!!"

Blowhole threw up his arms dramatically and Snot clapped wildly. He was the only one.

Hank J Twizzler spoke slowly with a surprisingly deep voice for a ten year old.

"So what's the plan?"

Blowhole's slithering tongue moistened his dry lips and his beady eyes shone like possessed jelly beans.

"It is a perfect plan. A plan which will ensure we become squadrillionaires overnight. I need your help and you need mine. I have created something every child on the planet will desire and every parent on the planet will pay handsomely for." He took a loud slurp from his mug and said, " — Downloadable Chocolate!"

The group looked around at each other's reactions, and each other's reaction was confusion.

"Downloadable chocolate!" repeated Blowhole in what he thought was a more villainous tone. "You will return to your countries and follow the instructions on these memory sticks which are being handed out by Snot. Download the coding onto your own computers and it will generate a candy virus which will infect every computer, laptop and e-phone within your territory. Every time every child logs on to their device they will automatically be directed to www.downloadablechocolate.com – where they will find irresistible HD images of chocolate all waiting to be e-tweaked and downloaded to their PCs. All for a very reasonable price!"

Flip Wrigley was turning the memory stick over in her hand and the idea over in her head.

"So, what do we get out of it?"

"Good question!" Blowhole turned to the whiteboard once more and clicked the remote. The screen filled with complex figures and profit projections. "By my calculations you will earn five million dollars each."

"And what do you get out of it?"

Blowhole's eyes twinkled like evil gobstoppers.

"Fame!" He could almost taste the word in his mouth. "Fame! I will have my name written in the history of confectionery alongside the inventor of cotton candy, the woman who unearthed nougat and the girl who first captured a gummi bear! I, Oleg Blowhole, will be known throughout the world as the inventor of Downloadable Chocolate – I will become King Candy! Oh and I'll earn a few million dollars too."

The international candy barons silently took in the enormity and audacity of the project. Their thoughts were broken by Herbert Dibdab.

"And what if we say no?"

Blowhole's upper lip trembled at the suggestion. His features formed the most villainous scowl he could muster and the room grew cold as he slowly hissed, "I'll tell your mummies and daddies all about you!"

Chapter Two
STUFF YOUR BEAR!

Maciii (pronounced Mac3) sat quietly on the school bus. His bright, fizzy blonde hair framed a face lost in concentration. Maciii was a brilliant kid, really brilliant. He could calculate one thousand positions of pi, think in seven dimensions and regularly came first in every (every!) school exam. Needless to say, everyone hated him. Luckily, he was usually so lost in thought he never noticed the snorts, tuts and pokes aimed at him. But this morning Maciii did notice something.

"We've stopped!" he announced.

"We've stopped!" echoed the Boggle twins behind him.

He hurried down the aisle of the bus avoiding a hail of spittle balls of paper and tapped the driver on the shoulder.

Tap-tap-tap. The shoulder belonged to Mr Clout, the dumpy, grumpy driver, who no one ever dared tap on the shoulder. Mr. Clout looked up in such amazement he was lost for words. A moment passed and he found one.

"What?"

"We've stopped!" repeated Maciii, tapping his watch with the most annoyingly clean finger Mr Clout had ever seen. The driver fumbled for another word.

"So?"

"Cosmology! I have to hand in an essay on cosmology!"

"Cosmology!" echoed the Boggle twins in the background.

"We're waiting for Joshua Bottleneck. New boy!" explained Mr Clout.

Maciii sighed and returned to his seat through a storm of pen tops.

The bus sat quietly putt-putt-putting as Maciii counted away the precious minutes when, suddenly, the doors of the bus hissed open and on board stepped a young boy of about Maciii's age but taller. He had an air of sophistication about him and a very well-ironed uniform. He surveyed the passengers, smiled briefly, and casually leaned against the door.

"First," he said in an educated and confident voice, "I'd like to say how dreadfully sorry I am for the lateness of my arrival. Terrible egg incident at brekkie. Had to completely rethink the outfit." He tugged at his cuffs and brushed his tie. "But I'm sure you'll agree it was well worth it."

He scanned a dazzling smile at the other passengers. "The name's Bottleneck, Joshua Bottleneck. Awful name.

I prefer to be called J.B. - Hello!"

Everyone found themselves saying, "Hello!" back.

J.B. looked about for a seat and glided over to Maciii.

"Spare?" he said, gesturing to the chair.

Maciii moved his school bag and J.B. slid into its place as the bus started to chug-chug-chug off. J.B. chose the moment to start a conversation.

"My name's…"

"Bottleneck, Joshua Bottleneck, but you prefer J.B. I heard!" snapped Maciii.

"I hope my lateness hasn't caused any incon…incon"

"Inconvenience?"

"That's the word!"

"Because of your tardiness, J.B., we're going to be late for school. I have an essay to hand in. The essay will be late which means minus marks and I never get minus marks."

"Awfully sorry!" said J.B. softly.

Maciii paused, looked at his companion and said, "I'm Maciii."

"Cool name. Is it real?"

"My real name is Edwin MacNaughton the Third, my father is Edwin MacNaughton the second and my grandfather…"

"Edwin MacNaughton the First?" J.B. grinned.

Maciii grinned back. "Good maths!"

The bus hummed with jabbering chatter as it chugged towards school.

"I've never met a Bottleneck before!" said Maciii.

"Ever heard of Jeremy Bottleneck, the world famous astrophysicist? That's my dad."

"Astrophysicist? OMG - can I meet him? I've got a great theory on the relative orbital co-ordinates of Cepheid variables. He'd love it!"

"Yes, yes, I'm sure he would. Wow! Look. A tree! What's your dad do?"

"Ermm…deep-sea diver, that sort of thing!"

"Wow!"

The school bus hissed to a halt outside the elementary school, as it did every day, every week, every year. But today was to be different. Very different.

Before the jabbering gaggle of kids could throng through the door, Miss Crumpley jumped aboard the bus. Miss Crumpley was a new teacher and like all new teachers she tried too hard and smiled far too often.

"Good morning, little boys and girls!" she beamed brightly. Everyone groaned, quietly.

"Stay in your seats, please. Pleasey-please. Bad news. I'm afraid our lovely little school has had to close today due to a terrible smell coming from the science lab. Some silly person has been doing naughty experiments after school and didn't open a window! The entire place stinks of rotten eggs!"

Everyone on the bus turned to Maciii and tutted.

"So that means we're lucky? Lucky, lucky, lucky! For today is a very special day! For today you will not be attending school!"

A huge cheer went up.

"Today you're going to go to work with your parents!"

The huge cheer went down.

Miss Crumpley shrugged and handed a sheaf of notes to

13

Mr Clout.

"Drop them off at these addresses, please. It's all been arranged." And then she was gone.

Mr Clout scratched his hat, sighed and put the bus back into gear.

Within fifteen minutes Maciii and J.B. found themselves deposited on the pavement in the middle of the busy town centre in front of a large, flashy sign which read, "Snugly Bug Teddy Factory – Stuff Your Bear!"

Maciii grasped the strap of his bag and pointed to the shop.

"I thought you said your dad…?" Maciii half-asked.

"I thought you said your dad…?" J.B. half-replied.

Then they weakly said in unison, "Works in a teddy bear factory!"

At that point a large bear with a pink bow tie appeared from the shop waving merrily.

"I'm Snugly Bug the Bear!" it chirpily announced. "Welcome to my shop!" and then it did a little skippy dance.

Maciii and J.B. sighed, shrugged and entered the shop. Snugly Bug giggled and followed them in.

The shop was a nauseating array of half-stuffed teddy bears. Teddy heads and legs hung around the place. Cute little costumes, Wellington boots and fluffy hats were laid out like a regular clothes shop, only for bears.

"I can't believe we've got to spend all day here." Maciii moaned, clonking his bag on the ground.

J.B.'s usual smile was starting to wither when his attention was caught by a hi-tech-looking teddy sitting on the counter with its pudgy arms open and a frozen grin on

14

its furry face. There was a small radio in its belly and without any prompting it suddenly chirped, "Hello! I'm Huggy Cub. Do you wuv me?"

"Well, we've only just met," said J.B., bemused.

"My name's Huggy Cub - what's yours?"

"I'm J.B.!"

"Hello, Jeremy. I'm Huggy Cub. Do you wuv me?"

Maciii had joined J.B. by the bear.

"Who are you?" asked the bear. Maciii looked about wondering how it had seen him.

"Edwin MacNaughton!"

The bear didn't reply.

"Edwin MacNaughton," Maciii repeated a little louder.

Suddenly, the bear's little arms started to rotate, its nose lit up and its tubby legs started to bang the counter.

"I think he likes you," laughed J.B.

Snugly Bug was suddenly by their side, pointing at the noisy bear.

"Did you do that?"

Maciii and J.B. looked at each other, unsure what to say. They quickly agreed on their response. They shrugged.

"I didn't realise who you were!" Snugly Bug grabbed their hands and led them through a large doorway neither had noticed before.

The large door in the large doorway led to a tiny, tatty, untidy office littered with papers and bits of injured teddies awaiting surgery.

"I am so sorry!" said Snugly Bug. "Do sit down!" He gestured with his furry paw in the direction of a pile of papers and bears. Maciii rummaged around, found a chair under a bear and sat. He wasn't sure what was happening but he could tell it would be more interesting than school. J.B. leaned casually against a filing cabinet, smiling.

"Let me say once again how sorry I am. We weren't expecting you!"

A telephone in the shape of a teddy next to Snugly Bug bleeped into life and he held it to his big furry ear.

"I know, I know, I know. I'm dealing with it right now. I thought they'd be taller, too! I've never met them before."

He slammed down the teddy-phone knocking over a pile of papers.

"Hang on a mo," he said, and started to unscrew his head. Underneath the teddy head was a human head. The head was bald, probably in its mid-forties and sweating a lot.

"Let me introduce myself," said the headless Snugly Bug. "My name is Captain Smitherington." He looked at Maciii. "Mr MacNaughton, this is a complete honour. It really is. I mean, gosh! And Mr Bottleneck, too. Gosh! I've heard so much about you!"

Maciii and J.B. exchanged a look somewhere between confusion and delight. They didn't know what was going on, but they were enjoying finding out.

"Better get you pair kitted out."

The bear with a human head ambled over to a cupboard, threw open the doors and scrabbled about inside. He re-emerged, sweating some more and clutching some interesting objects.

"Flak jackets! These should fit. Able to withstand 100 pounds of pressure p.s.i." He clumped two heavy black jackets on the desk.

"P.s.i!" J.B. repeated, without a clue what it meant.

"Now then - splodgers!"

He produced two short, black tubes each with triggers and handles.

"High velocity, stunning accuracy. Produces a constant barrage of 100% splodge!"

"100%!" said J.B., still impressed. He wasn't sure what he was being impressed by, but felt impressed nonetheless.

Maciii sat silently trying to calibrate the strange goings-on that were going-on. The only thing he knew for certain was Snugly Bug had mistaken J.B. and himself for someone else. But who were the someone elses?

"Exercise commencing in Minus One Minute!" announced Smitherington, looking at the teddy clock once more. "Final equipment – goggles! Okay, kit-up!"

J.B was about to ask a question, but decided it might spoil the fun, so they put on the flak jackets and goggles and took their splodgers.

"Looking rather smart!" said J.B., admiring himself in a pink teddy mirror.

Smitherington tweaked the ear of a battered bear and the cupboard slid silently to one side revealing a glistening elevator. He gestured towards it.

"What happens next?" asked Maciii.

Smitherington smiled admiringly. "As if you didn't know!"

Maciii and J.B. shrugged at each other and entered. As they turned back they saw Smitherington saluting. "It's an honour, sirs. Welcome back to MI3(and a bit)!" and the door closed in front of his beaming face.

The elevator was quiet. Maciii was quieter still. J.B. finally said,

"I have no idea what's going on."

"Me neither, but I think we're about to find out!" replied Maciii, and the elevator slowly began to descend.

Chapter Three
NOTHING!

J.B. brushed fluff from his flak jacket and looked at Maciii as they waited silently in the bright elevator. He started to hum softly and then hovered his fingers by the buttons, considering whether to push one.

"Don't!" whispered Maciii. J.B. didn't.

There was a sudden whirring and clicking sound and the door slid open revealing…

"Nothing!" Maciii pointed out pointlessly.

"And lots of it!" agreed J.B., looking around.

All they could hear was the sound of their own nervous breathing, when out of the darkness a voice hissed, "Night vision!" and the lights in the elevator snapped off.

Maciii had already noticed the small switch on the side of the goggles and swiftly clicked it, then clicked J.B.'s. Both their eyes quickly adjusted to the strange vision given by the goggles. The darkness remained darkish but shapes took shape all around them. Odd shapes, all pale green in colour. Maciii could make out a flat-looking tree and behind that an even flatter bush.

"It's a mock-up of a forest environment!" he concluded.

"Cool!" replied J.B., looking at his pale green hand. "What do we do with it?"

Maciii tentatively placed a foot forward on to the ground. J.B. closely followed. Suddenly, the elevator door smoothly slid shut behind them.

"I think we're alone," Maciii said tensely

"We can't both be alone," whispered J.B. "I mean if I were alone you wouldn't be here and if you were alone I wouldn't be here, but I am and you are, so we're not."

"Brilliant logic, J.B.!"

Suddenly, a greenish figure ran across within inches of them.

"I don't think we're alone!" yelped Maciii. There was a sudden flash and bang from J.B.'s direction, followed by a splattering sound, which was followed by a dribbling sound.

"I think I've splodged myself!" whimpered J.B. "I bought these trousers in Harrods the other day. Maciii? Maciii?" But his new friend had moved forward leaving J.B. no choice but to follow.

As they cautiously stepped into the deeper darkness, new shapes emerged. Suddenly a frozen face snapped into view - a sneering face with slick black hair. A voice rattled out,

"So, you think you can beat me, do you? Well, take that!"

From out of nowhere a splodgy missile whistled towards the boys. Maciii deftly dodged it, but J.B. didn't.

"I've been splodged again!" he moaned. "Harrods' best trousers!"

Maciii raised his splodger and took aim. He felt for the trigger and slowly squeezed. A thundering gob of blue splodge burst from the spout and hit the sneering image straight in its smug face. There was a tinny fanfare and the face was replaced with a shiny number 7. A voice announced, "Seven points!"

Both suddenly realised what they had to do. "Let's splodge!" they both cried and launched into a splattering barrage of splodging. Soggy globs whistled through the darkness, past their ears, eyes and, occasionally, knees. J.B. was hit once, twice, three times.

"Harrods!" he bellowed into the darkness and splodged wildly at nothing.

Maciii was picking his targets with more care and precision and his points were clocking up.

"17!" announced the voice.

They crept further into the darkness, ready to strike the next target. Something rustled to J.B.'s left and he whirled round. A full-face photo close-up of Maciii lit up and J.B. aimed at it.

"No!" shouted Maciii.

"No!" cried J.B., lowering his splodger.

"Think! Splodge that and we lose points!"

They moved slowly forward once more and a huge picture popped into vision. It was the face of a woman of about sixty, a severe look in her eyes and a stern look in her nose. Think of the nastiest head teacher you can imagine, then add a bit more nastiness. That's her.

It didn't take J.B and Maciii long to decide whether it was friend or foe.

"Fire!" shouted Maciii, and round after round of squidgy gunge slapped into the frowning face.

"Exercise aborted! Exercise aborted! Exercise aborted!" the tinny voice chanted. Suddenly, lights were clicking on all over the place revealing a slick, white cellar with cut-out trees and bushes. J.B and Maciii sloshed the remaining splodge from their faces and flicked up their goggles. A female face was staring down at them. It was a face with a severe look in its eyes and a stern look in its nose and it wasn't a photograph.

"Whatever do you think you're playing at?" asked a voice which was even more severe and stern than its face and nose. "MacNaughton? Bottleneck?" The woman was tweedily dressed with patches on her elbows and knees and shoulders and she was clearly not to be messed with.

Maciii and J.B shrugged their shrug and wondered what she would say next.

"You're fired!" was what she said next.

From the far end of the room, Smitherington, now dressed in the shirt and tie of an office worker, hurried over, tugging off his teddy paws as he approached.

"If I may interject here, Colonel, I think there may have been a slight error."

Maciii and J.B. exchanged a quizzical glance on the word 'Colonel'.

The Colonel turned and looked at Smitherington as if he were an irritating fly.

"Error?"

"Computer error, I mean, not my error! I'm quite new so haven't had time to make any errors," his blabbering voice stuttered to a halt and he softly added. "These are not Agents MacNaughton and Bottleneck."

"Then who are they?" she spluttered.

Smitherington fiddled with his tie.

"Smitherington!!!!??" Her bellow made a light bulb vibrate at the far end of the room.

"These are…" he dropped his voice to the lowest of low whispers, "…Their sons."

The Colonel looked like a zit about to pop.

"Their sons?!!!??"

"It appears J.B. registered with the desktop ID teddy and the voice interpreter thought he'd said Jeremy which is the name of his father, Agent Jeremy Bottleneck. And MacNaughton logged on as MacNaughton, but he is MacNaughton the third, not MacNaughton the second which is the name of our agent. Computer error, you see?"

Maciii had been standing quietly trying to work out what this was all about when a thought popped into his mind. He recalled what Smitherington had said to them as they stepped into the lift.

"MI3(and a bit)!" he said quietly. "This is Military Intelligence 3(and a bit). The teddy shop is just a fake front! Our fathers are secret agents!"

J.B. smiled broadly, nodded slowly and said, "I don't get it!"

Maciii was about to explain it all when the Colonel broke in.

"You have now seen the inner workings of our top secret hush-hush operation. And as we're no longer allowed to scan and erase memories, I'm afraid we're stuck with a problem…and quite a big problem."

There was a long pause as all four considered the situation. J.B was the first to speak.

"I still don't get it!"

The Colonel started pacing up and down, back and forth, forth and back, closely followed by Smitherington who was doing his best thinking face.

"They were very good at the exercise though, Colonel, and we could use undercover children in some capacity, I'm sure"

"What capacity?"

Smitherington looked about the room for inspiration. He needed to redeem the situation, impress the boss and dig himself out of this huge hole. His eager eyes fell on the picture of Oleg Blowhole with its slick black hair as a dribble of splodge trickled down its frozen features. A smile stretched over Smitherington's lips and he tugged at the Colonel's sleeve.

"What about Operation Blowhole?" he said, raising his eyebrows in what he thought was an irresistible manner.

The Colonel grated her teeth, thought, then suddenly whooped, "Brilliant!" and Smitherington sighed a silent sigh of relief. The Colonel turned her happy face to the expectant faces of Maciii and J.B.

"Boys, have you ever heard of a school called St Smugg's?"

Chapter Four
"I'M GOING TO PUKE!"

The chopping 'copter blades of the F13 Da Vinci Mk 2 sliced the chill air above the Snugly Bug Teddy Factory. The shiny black fuselage was ready to soar into the sky any second. Only one thing was stopping it.

"I'm going to puke!"

"It's okay," said Maciii, as gently as he could over the growling howl of the engine. "Flying in a helicopter is statistically safer than crossing a road!"

"I want to cross a road!" squawked J.B., trying to unbuckle his seatbelt. "Let me out! I want to cross a road!"

The pilot's voice clicked into their headphones.

"Welcome aboard today's top secret flight to St Smugg's

Very Private School. Today we'll be flying at an altitude of about…oh, I don't know…it'll probably go up and down a lot. Oh, I wonder what that little button does…"

"Captain Mole, behave!" The Colonel's voice cut the air louder than the rotor blades and the pilot mumbled something about not being allowed to have any fun.

"Junior Agents Maciii and J.B., you have both been well briefed and today we will be initiating Operation Blowhole. The flight will take approximately two hours!"

"How did we get ourselves into this mess?" squeaked J.B., holding his hand in front of his mouth as the helicopter lurched from the ground and headed skyward.

The mess into which they had got themselves began exactly three days before when their identities were mistaken at the Snugly Bug Teddy Factory. Since then they had been on an intense training course at the MI3(and a bit) Headquarters. They had been sworn in as junior MI3(and a bit) agents, been issued with some top-line gadgetry only Maciii really understood, and they had been given a vital, PowerPoint demonstration by the Colonel about their target – Oleg Blowhole.

"A boy capable of immense naughtiness!" the Colonel had warned as she struggled with the laptop in the briefing room two days earlier. She had snorted and handed it to Smitherington.

"Oleg Blowhole!" she continued, striding around the tables. "Eleven years old, parentage uncertain, but currently studying at St Smugg's School, fees paid by an anonymous source thought to be a millionaire industrialist. At nine he was responsible for the infamous Lego Trafficking Scandal providing Lego to Third World countries at over-inflated prices. At nine and a half sold fake farting cushion apps on e-phone. At nine and three quarters narrowly avoided arrest after being caught with a consignment of two hundred unlicensed yo-yos. As you can see, a very dangerous boy!"

Maciii was drumming his bored fingers on the desk. "So how do we fit in?" he asked.

J.B., whose mind had wandered as it often did, was staring out of the window. A helicopter flew past overhead and he thought, "I'd never go up in one of those!" but his mouth said "Yeah, how do we fit in?"

"You are the same age. The same level of intelligence." She glanced briefly at J.B. "Almost. And you are now Agents of MI3(and a bit). You are to be flown to St Smugg's where you will infiltrate Blowhole's network and discover whatever you can."

"So what's this fellow up to at the moment?" asked J.B in a moment of clarity.

"We believe he's getting heavily involved in confectionery. Sweets, chocolate, toffee, caramel. We're not entirely sure, but he has recently held a meeting with some of the most dangerous candy dealers on the planet! We believe he may be planning his biggest scam to date!"

A hundred and one questions whizzed through Maciii's brain as he calculated everything he was hearing. But only one question mattered.

"But how does an eleven-year-old boy manage to do all this?"

Smitherington was jabbing at the laptop with a pen as the Colonel drew back a chair and sat down.

"Good question. Blowhole's operations are well funded. Three months ago we dispatched Agent Brookfield to pose as the school caretaker. He wasn't there long when his cover was blown by, erm, the real school caretaker. There was a fight over mops and cleaning fluids and we had to pull him out. However, in the short time he was there he managed to access Blowhole's quarters and record this footage…"

She turned to Smitherington who cheerfully said, "Nearly ready, ma'am!"

"It seems Blowhole controls his entire empire from a multi-functional, web-fed, mobile-control throne. It is golden and in the shape of…in the shape of…Smitherington, you take over here…"

Smitherington looked up brightly from the computer. "Bottom!"

"Yes, that's the word."

"Bum, butt, arse…"

"That's enough!"

Smitherington punched a button on the keyboard and onto the screen shimmered some raw digital footage of a huge white room dominated by a huge white table. The camera prowled around until it finally spotted a huge, golden throne which could easily seat three people. The camera circled the throne showing that it did, indeed, look like a bottom and quite a flabby one. The camera focused on the arms which were covered with tiny buttons, joysticks and touch pads. A set of headphones sat on the seat, and a remote control with more buttons than Maciii had ever seen was thrown carelessly to one side. On the soundtrack all that could be heard was Brookfield's nervous breathing when suddenly, far in the background, a voice shouted, "Brookfield! It's toilet time!" and the film abruptly stopped.

"And what's this machine called?" asked Maciii, slowly.

The Colonel leaned closer to the faces of Maciii and J.B. and spoke softly but firmly, "Goldenbum!"

J.B., who had been listening on and off throughout the conversation and had taken in most of what was said, suddenly had a thought. He pondered and wondered for a moment, then decided to put his wondering into words.

"Did you say we'd be flying?"

St Smugg's Very Private School sprawled out on the beach like a well-groomed, overweight sunbather, smugly showing off its pristine white walls to every passing seagull. Flags from at least thirty different nations fluttered loudly above the stainless steel gates. And as the F13 Da Vinci Mk 2 swooped out of the sun, a flurry of excited young people rushed from every classroom to welcome the newcomers. Maciii counted 231 children in the playground.

"I didn't puke!" whooped J.B. as the 'copter touched down a little harder than he expected. J.B. held his mouth, Maciii held his breath.

"I didn't puke again!"

The newly appointed junior agents both stared out of the window at their welcome. Two long lines of pupils formed a corridor leading from the 'copter to the main building, and on the steps of the school entrance stood two welcoming figures – one an adult and the other a pupil.

"And those are the people you need to befriend!" announced the Colonel, fiddling with the door lock.

She snorted a short snort at Smitherington who also

29

fiddled with the lock, who then snorted at Captain Mole who did a bit of fiddling himself but failed to open the door. The Colonel waved a queenly hand at the lines of freshly ironed uniforms and freshly scrubbed faces, then smacked a queenly hand across Smitherington's head.

"Get it open!" she hissed.

"This is state of the art, infrared, motion-detecting, dual-locking central security!" Captain Mole hissed back, dodging a queenly smack.

"And what's wrong with it?"

"I think the battery's flat!"

All five of the 'copter passengers started pressing their combined weight against the door and with a crack and a crash and a couple of unexpected hiccups all five passengers tumbled from the 'copter into a scrambling heap of arms, legs, teeth and Military Intelligence-issue knickers.

"Mother!" shouted Maciii, lifting the Colonel to her knees, her thighs and finally her feet. This was their cover story. Maciii and J.B. were the adopted sons of Mrs. Squidge - a name accidentally inflicted on them when the school secretary asked Smitherington the family name of the new pupils. He panicked when he realised he hadn't thought of one and quickly thought of one – Squidge.

"Mrs Squidge!" said a very well educated and refined sounding voice, but with the tiniest hint of nerves. The voice belonged to the mouth of Sir Otto Gripe – Head Teacher of St Smugg's. He was an odd-shaped man who looked like he'd decided to stop growing taller around the age of ten and had concentrated all his attention on growing wider. He giggled slightly.

"You seem to have fallen..." he giggled some more, "from the..." he giggled again, "...from the..." He slipped a red handkerchief from his pocket and covered his giggles with it. "Allow me to have the finest honour of kindly introducing myself to yourself. I am Sir Otto Gripe, MA, TT, BxC, and I have the undoubted and glorious honour of being head teacher of the best school in the world – St Smugg's!"

And with that he fluttered his red handkerchief and 231 young voices chanted.

"St Smugg's!"

And Sir Otto Gripe giggled again.

"These are my adopted children, Joshua and Edward Squidge," said the Colonel, readjusting everything that could be readjusted and recovering her composure. "They prefer to be called J.B. and Maciii. I want only the best for my boys!"

"Then I can think of no better way for them to achieve the best than by placing them in the hands of our finest head boy, Oleg Blowhole!" he announced, and fluttered his handkerchief.

"Oleg Blowhole!" chanted 231 voices.

"That's enough!" shouted Sir Otto at the 231 eager faces.

"That's enough!" they echoed.

"Perhaps I could intervene here!" the voice slithered from the lips of Oleg Blowhole as he gingerly but firmly pushed the head teacher aside and fixed J.B. and Maciii with a welcoming but deadly stare. "I am Oleg Blowhole, head boy, and I would consider it an honour to introduce you to the finest school in the world! May I take your luggage?"

J.B. and Maciii handed their suitcases to Blowhole who handed them to Snot who looked like he would be rummaging through them the moment he was alone, and that's exactly what he was planning.

"I'll allow you to say goodbye to your family and then I'll show you around!"

Maciii and J.B. kissed their 'mother', patted Smitherington and Mole then followed Blowhole.

Despite having the legs of an eleven year old, Oleg Blowhole strode the corridors of St Smugg's like a mighty general pacing his field of battle, and in many ways it was his field of battle. Snot scuttled and sweated behind, struggling with the luggage.

"I am head boy!" he trilled as Maciii and J.B followed behind. "Whatever I say happens, whatever I say goes. Got it?"

They got it. In fact, they got a lot more than Blowhole realised. "Oh, and I almost forgot…" he said, coming to a halt. "This is Snot!" He gestured at his sneering servant, who grunted and tried to wave. J.B. and Maciii couldn't help noticing his odd nose.

"I know. Horrible, isn't it? His nose got cut off many years back in a terrible sushi chopping incident," Blowhole explained. "The surgeon worked hard to reattach it. Unfortunately, the hospital trolley was the wrong way round and poor Snot's nose was reattached upside down, wasn't it, Snotty? Whenever he goes out in the rain he has to wear a wide-brimmed hat in case he drowns. And whenever he sneezes he has to remember to wipe his forehead. Show them around, Snot!"

"I thought you were going to show us around?" said Maciii, softly. Blowhole turned on the spot and looked at him like something unexpected he'd found wriggling in his ear.

"As I think I explained, I am head boy. I have very important things to do! You're not going to be a problem, are you?"

J.B. and Maciii both shook their heads and decided to say nothing.

Blowhole looked them up and down and back again and finally said, "Good! Drinks in my room tonight at 8! Don't think of being late!" And with that he strode off leaving the two boys with Snot and the luggage.

After swiftly unpacking their bags, which they had managed to wrestle from Snot's grip, J.B. and Maciii quickly showered, changed into some respectable evening wear as supplied by MI3(and a bit) and soon found themselves at 7.59pm (according to Maciii's atomically accurate wristwatch) standing before the door which led to the room of their target, Oleg Blowhole.

"So what do you think of it so far?" asked Maciii.

"Well, these socks don't go with this tie!" replied J.B., checking his reflection in a stained-glass window.

"About the case, doofus!" Maciii was warming to J.B. but he just wished he focused a bit more.

"Doofus? That's a kind of tropical fruit, right?" when the door squeaked and squealed open and the pompous face and the inverted nose of Snot poked out.

"Yeeeeeeees?" his voice sounded like a washing

machine on its final cycle.

Maciii pointed at himself and J.B. and nodded pleasantly hoping the penny would drop. The penny stayed where it was.

"Yeeeeeeees?"

"Hi, I'm J.B. and this is my friend, Maciii. We met this afternoon?"

"I have no idea who you are!" the boy said haughtily and began to close the door. Suddenly, his face grimaced, twitched, juddered and he squeaked like a startled otter.

Someone behind him was cuffing him around the neck and muttering,

"On a scale of one to ten, how stupid are you, Snot?" said the voice behind the door. "These are my guests. Let them in. Not straight away – wait until I get under my spotlight!"

Snot stared at J.B. and Maciii with sighing eyes and whistled soundlessly to himself until he heard,

"Now!"

Suddenly Snot's eyes lit up.

"Mr Maciii and and Mr J.B., how lovely to see you once more. Do come in."

And with that Snot threw open the massive door to reveal the inside of Oleg Blowhole's domain.

Everything in the room (everything!) was made of chocolate. The floor was a rich, brown chocolate. The chairs were carved from chocolate, the desk dominating the room was a huge slab of dark chocolate. Telephone: chocolate, TV: chocolate. Even the paintings on the walls were chocolate.

Maciii was amazed by what he saw and so was J.B. a few seconds later. Sitting in a sleek, chocolate chair on the far side of the room under a dim spotlight was Oleg Blowhole. He was casually drinking some hot chocolate from a mug made of chocolate which looked like it could melt at any moment.

Snot coughed and announced "Mr and Mr…!"

"Yes, I know who they are, doofus!" snapped Blowhole, placing his mug to one side and approaching the boys.

J.B. patted Snot on the shoulder as he passed saying "Tropical fruit!" Snot look confused and scurried away.

Blowhole slowly shook each boy's hand and stared deep into his eyes as if he was trying to read their minds. Maciii's mind was like a giant encyclopaedia; J.B.'s was more like a short leaflet on windsurfing.

"Welcome to my world. Stand and admire it. I know what you're thinking!" he said smiling at J.B., then realised he'd no idea what J.B. was thinking as J.B. was smiling at a teapot. "I know what you're thinking…" he said moving to Maciii. "You're thinking what a strange room!"

Maciii was about to reply when Blowhole added.

"You're thinking – how come everything is made of chocolate?"

Maciii was about to reply when Blowhole added,

"You're thinking – who in their right mind would build a room out of chocolate?"

Maciii was about to reply when Blowhole added,

"You're thinking – why is everything made of chocolate? That's what you're thinking, isn't it?"

"No…" answered Maciii, "I was thinking how do you

stop it from melting on a hot day like today?"

Blowhole turned on the spot and tried to size up the new boy. Clearly, the taller one was no real challenge. Might be useful in a rumble, but intellectually no contest. The short one, though, might well prove a problem.

A smile slid across Blowhole's face.

"Perceptive question, Maciii. I can see we are going to get on brilliantly. Air-con is the answer. Top of the range air conditioning, which instantly responds to atmospheric conditions and adjusts the room temperature accordingly. So my precious chocolate will never, ever melt!"

Blowhole moved over to J.B. who was still admiring the chocolate teapot.

"Swiss, original cocoa bean, 1967. Worth a fortune on the open market. Tell me, J.B., do you tiddle?"

Before J.B. could even consider a possible answer, Maciii stepped in.

"I don't think we know what you mean by tiddle, Blowhole."

And with that Blowhole slapped a chocolate button on his desk and there was a buzzing and a whirring and the entire top of the desk rotated revealing a huge chocolate-playing surface in the centre of which was a large chocolate cup.

"Tiddlywinks, Mr Maciii! An old St Smugg's tradition. Could I challenge you to a game?" He produced a bag of chocolate counters and tossed them towards Maciii who snatched them out of the air, even impressing himself. Blowhole tried to hide a sneer as he said, "I'll take that as a yes!" He moved very, very close until Maciii could sniff the whiff of hot chocolate on his bated breath and said in a dark tone, "I must tell you - I'm a champion winker!"

The lights in the room dimmed even further than the dim light that was already dimmed and all attention focused on the game.

Blowhole placed his counters on the table and leaned over them like a heron about to snatch a goldfish. With one well-practised click he sent his counter spiralling through the air, then it landed with a click in the chocolate cup.

"That's one tiddle to me, Mr Maciii!" he announced brightly, and offered Maciii the board. "So what brings you to St Smugg's?"

Maciii was cautiously lining up his shot. "Education!" he said, flatly.

"Really? You must be one of the few people ever to come to St Smugg's for education!"

Maciii flipped his counter and sent it sailing through the air to land with a disappointing slap on the floor.

"Minus one tiddle to you, Maciii!"

"What do you mean?" asked Maciii.

"Because you missed you lose a tiddle!" said J.B. who had grasped the gist of the game surprisingly quickly.

"No, I mean about the education!" corrected Maciii.

Blowhole was judging the distance between his next counter and the cup.

"For many years now St Smugg's has had a growing reputation for attracting children of parents whose businesses are not…how shall we say…on the right side of the law."

"I knew that!" said Maciii, even though he knew that

already he wanted to appear like someone who didn't know it trying to appear like they did.

Blowhole assessed his reaction and concluded Maciii knew nothing.

"Criminals have been sending their children here for years!" He clicked his counter and it tumbled through the air landing with the same precision as its predecessor. "And are your parents in the villainy trade?"

Maciii considered his answer carefully and was about to speak when J.B. said,

"Yes, yes, they are actually!"

"And what do your parents do?"

"Well," said J.B., making the 'well' last as long as he could without looking like he was making up the next bit, "They steal…" he thought some more,"…paper clips!" J.B. nodded brightly at Maciii, who inside his head was slapping the outside of his head.

"Your tiddle!"

Maciii aimed another counter and missed once again. "Oh, how unfortunate!"

"And what about Sir Otto?"

"Oh, him? He's a complete buffoon, total doofus!"

J.B. looked confused.

"He knows nothing. I run St Smugg's. I have total control of everything! And that's why I enjoy meeting all the newcomers personally. I'm head boy!" Another of Blowhole's counters tumbled into its target. "Of course, if anyone interfered with my operations, if anyone so much as tinkered with my plans, if anyone tried to muscle in on my doings - I'd break them in two as if they were a little chocolate counter!" he said, breaking in two a little chocolate counter to make his point. "I think our game is over!"

"But you haven't given me a chance to win!"

"I never give anyone a chance to win, Mr Maciii!" Blowhole and Maciii were once more face to face. Maciii was weighing up his next move, Blowhole was weighing up his opponent and J.B. was weighing up the teapot.

"Great teapot!" said J.B. breaking the atmosphere and nearly breaking the teapot. Suddenly, the doorbell dingle-ingled breaking the already broken atmosphere.

"Bell!" hissed Blowhole moving away from the confrontation and slapping the chocolate button hiding the tiddlywinks table once more. "Snot! Snot! Snot, bell, Snot!"

Snot was at the door within seconds and opened it to reveal two of St Smugg's most notorious pupils. Samantha Clunk frothed into the room like a cork exploding from a champagne bottle.

"Blowhole, darling, thank you so much for inviting us!" She flapped her pink wrap like a sneezing flamingo and Snot removed it from her shoulders unveiling evening wear which looked like it had just walked off a Parisian catwalk. Samantha twirled displaying the dress saying, "Tabby Chic! Isn't it marvellous?"

J.B. was about to introduce himself when Maciii blocked his way and whispered, "Tabby Chic is the name of her dress!"

J.B. couldn't understand why a dress needed a name and wondered if it came when she called.

"We?" asked Blowhole, suspiciously.

"I brought Deeky!" Clunk shrieked.

Blowhole's smile flipped back and forth trying to stop itself becoming a sneer.

"How lovely!" he said, clearly thinking the opposite. From the door a small boy of a similar age to Clunk quietly padded. He was staring at the floor, not because he'd seen anything interesting there but because he hated making eye contact. He was dressed in jeans and T-shirt with an obscure maths formula across the front. Maciii shook his hand.

"I'm Maciii – isn't that the mathematical formula for Einstein's Special Theory of Relativity?"

The boy raised his eyes from the floor.

"I'm Dwayne Deek – yes, it certainly is."

J.B. moved over to Clunk.

"Squidge!"

"Clunk!"

"Now if I could have your attention. If the host of this evening's events could just have…hello?"

All four of the guests turned to their host.

"Good!" Blowhole coughed, ran his hand through his slick black hair and nailed his guests with a sinister stare. "Tonight is the night!"

"Hurrah!" clapped Clunk. "What for?"

"Tonight I launch the first advertising campaign for my ultimate scheme – Downloadable Chocolate!"

Clunk clapped again.

"Maciii and J.B., you are fortunate to witness the unveiling of the most audacious moneymaking plan in the history of world confectionery. Downloadable chocolate will soon be gushing out of laptops and PCs throughout the world – thanks to the power of Goldenbum!"

And with that he gestured dramatically to the balcony of his room and Snot dramatically tried to throw open the French window.

"I think I've snagged something!" he muttered, tugging at a curtain. There was a rip and the door flew open. Blowhole beckoned to his guests to follow him out.

The night sky was drawing in and twinkling stars winked down on the beautiful island. There on the balcony was Goldenbum. Maciii recognised it from the footage shown them at the briefing. It seemed even more shiny and expensive looking than he remembered. Bleeping, shining lights bleeped and shone, and on the small monitor a screen saver wriggled through its programme. Cables streamed from the machine and a purring fan softly cooled a million and one circuits.

"If I am to become a multi-millionaire – and there's no reason why not – then the population of the world needs to know of my product, and this is how!"

Snot slipped him a remote control, Blowhole stabbed a button and Goldenbum suddenly bleeped into virtual activity. The lights grew shinier, the screen saver wriggled from the monitor to be replaced by a scroll of rolling formulas and DOS commands. The cooling fan growled like an arrogant tiger.

Blowhole scanned his enwrapped audience and stabbed another button. Slowly the entire machine started to tilt on its golden legs and the most bum-like part rose and pointed heavenwards. It was mooning the moon. Blowhole pressed yet another button and with a blinding flash a piercing yellow light shone from the base of the bum and shot out towards the stars.

"Goldenbum, lady and gentlemen!" But all three guests – and even Snot – were too stunned to applaud. Stunned beyond words for the blinding light was projecting a message across the surface of the moon! Every human across the northern hemisphere of the planet that dark, clear night could read the words emblazoned there. And what they could read was –

"DOWNLOADABLE CHOCOLATE™ coming to a candy store near you – from Blowhole Enterprises!"

"There!" said Blowhole, quietly. "That should stir up a bit of interest!"

Chapter Five
INCORRECT PASSWORD

Within two nanoseconds of the advert for DOWNLOADABLE CHOCOLATE™ being splattered across the unsuspecting face of the moon, almost everyone on the planet wanted to know about it. Within three nanoseconds almost every phone was texting texts like "What's DOWNLOADABLE CHOCOLATE™?", "Where can I get DOWNLOADABLE CHOCOLATE™?", "How do you spell DONLODIBL CHOKOLAT™?" And within four nanoseconds almost every tip-tap-typing finger across the globe was inputting the words DOWNLOADABLE CHOCOLATE™ into sites like Gurgle, Ikipedi and Twitface. As Blowhole predicted, it had created a 'bit' of interest.

But neither Blowhole nor Snot was taking the slightest bit of notice of the global reaction, because as this chapter begins each is tucked up in their respective beds, one snoring like a baby the other snoring like a baby seal.

On the balcony Goldenbum hummed quietly to itself, analysing thousands of texts and emails as they fizzed and whizzed around the world. Any text, email, RSS or blog containing the words 'Downloadable', 'Chocolate' or 'Blowhole' was instantly logged in Goldenbum's staggering 101010 K RAM memory for future use.

And inside Blowhole's quarters two shadowy figures, who should have been stalking across the room like well-trained panthers, were bumping into furniture like well-stupid chickens.

"Why didn't you charge up the night goggles?" hissed the irritated voice of the shorter figure.

"My mistake. Put my e-phone on charge instead if that's any use. Maybe not!" explained the voice of the taller figure.

"Well, let's wait for our eyes to adjust to the darkness…"

"Ouch!"

"Which means standing still!"

"Yeah, still, okay."

As Maciii's eyes slowly adjusted to the darkness, he got a better view of J.B. who was standing next to him with his eyes closed.

"Why are your eyes closed?"

"I don't like the dark!" whispered J.B.

Maciii decided to focus on the prime reason for the break in.

"Okay!" said Maciii, taking charge. "This is what's going to happen. I'm going to hack into Goldenbum and find out what I can. You are going to keep look out. Okay?"

"Okay!"

"You may want to open your eyes to do it!"

But J.B. didn't reply, as his phone was vibrating. He slipped it from his pocket and its dim glow lit up his face

"Text! From Grandpa Steve. Wants to know where to get Downloaded Chocolate!" J.B. said brightly.

"Give me the phone!" hissed Maciii.

J.B. reluctantly handed it over and within seconds Maciii was hunched over Goldenbum's keyboard choosing which key to press like someone picking their favourite sweet from a tray. J.B. was peeking out of a crack in the door.

"Now what would be Blowhole's password?" Maciii wondered to himself and tried a few taps.

INCORRECT PASSWORD

"It's the little guy I'm looking out for, right?" whispered J.B.

"Blowhole."

"And the guy with the ear?"

"Nose! I need to concentrate – just keep a look out!"

And Maciii started pecking at keys with the speed of an expert, but each peck failed to break through the security barrier.

INCORRECT PASSWORD
INCORRECT PASSWORD
INCORRECT PASSWORD
FINAL ATTEMPT BEFORE SHUT DOWN

Maciii paused, nibbled a nail and pondered. What could

it be?

His thoughts were shattered by another question from J.B.

"The little guy's name is Snot?"

"Yes, Snot."

"Wow! Who could forget a name like Snot?"

Maciii clicked his fingers and almost yelped as a little light bulb lit up in his head.

"Snot!"

He poked the four letters in the keyboard and pressed 'Enter'.

Goldenbum purred happily and its screen saver faded to be replaced by a colourful site map with endless options.

"We're in!" hissed Maciii across the room. "This is amazing! There is so much information here. All we need do is download these files, encrypt them and send them to MI3(and a bit)! This could really nail Blowhole!"

Maciii swivelled back to Goldenbum and hunched over the keyboard once more. He was about to start tip-tapping when the screen suddenly flipped over to a flashing red warning…

ABORT AIR.CON.?

QUIT OR EXECUTE?

The stale blue light lit up Maciii's confused face. How did that come up? He tapped some more keys, but the message remained. He stopped clicking the keyboard but continued to hear tapping.

"What's that noise? What are you doing?"

"Texting!"

"Who? Why? I mean, now?"

"Back to Grandpa Steve!"

Maciii's silent sighs were getting louder and louder and he sighed the loudest silent sigh he'd so far sighed.

"Can we please concentrate…wait a minute. You just gave me your phone!"

Maciii could almost hear J.B. nodding in the darkness.

"So what are you tapping on?"

Maciii almost shrieked as he realised what was happening. He leapt from his chair and stumbled over to J.B., caught his shoe under the chocolate carpet and fell face first.

"You okay?" asked J.B., peering into the darkness.

There was no reply so J.B. shrugged and clicked a final button.

"Don't…press…send!" Maciii groaned from the floor. "You're holding the remote control for Goldenbum!"

"Oh…" said J.B.

They both turned to the screen and saw the word 'Execute' light up and fade. High above the room the piping piping chilling cold air, which preserved Blowhole's precious chocolate, clicked and clunked off. A small red light flashed on the keyboard, and Maciii and J.B braced themselves for the forthcoming ear-shattering alarm bell.

And they waited some more.

They waited a tiny bit longer.

But none came.

J.B. sighed a loud sigh of relief and offered Maciii a hi-five.

"Why is your hand sticky?" he asked.

J.B. sniffed his hand and concluded, "Chocolate.

Belgian, I think. Nice and fruity!"

Maciii smacked his hand to his forehead.

"The chocolate's melting. The process has already started!"

"I think it's time to execute MI3(and a bit) Directive 79a sub-clause 15x!" announced Maciii

"What's MI3(and a bit) Directive 79a sub-clause 15x?" asked J.B.

"When confronted by insurmountable problems – quickly get the heck out of there!" yelped J.B.

And the heck out of there they quickly got.

At 3am the next morning Maciii was snatched from his dreams of particle physics, and at 3.01am J.B. was snatched from his dreams of happy ducks by a sneering, leering voice they both slowly recognised as Snot's.

"Who's been naughty little boys, then?" he hissed in their half-waking ears, which he then grabbed, and pulled them out of bed.

"Argghhh!" groaned Maciii.

"Owwwww!" moaned J.B.

Before either knew what was happening, they had stumbled and tumbled out of bed and were being frogmarched down a dark corridor. But where were they going?

"Where are we going?" asked Maciii.

The answer was written across the door on which Snot's knobbly knuckle was now knocking.

SIR OTTO GRIPE, DO COME IN

Snot threw open the creaking door and hurled his victims

onto the floor of Gripe's pristine, book-riddled office.

"As you requested!" snarled Snot, proudly.

Maciii and J.B found themselves staring at two pairs of slippered feet. One pair were junior size and the other probably those of an adult, Maciii quickly deduced. He peered up past the pyjama-clad legs and into the grimacing faces of Blowhole and Sir Otto Gripe.

"Oh, diddley-diddley-dear!" said Sir Otto, snatching a handkerchief from his pyjama pocket and dabbing his forehead.

"Hello, new boys!" Blowhole's smile looked like it was going to snap off his face in delight. "Sit!"

Snot shoved a couple of chairs roughly against Maciii and J.B. and they clambered onto them.

"So you think it's them?" asked Gripe, nervously fluttering his hanky in the general direction of the boys.

"I know it's them, Gripe!" Blowhole started to slowly circle the chairs. "Do you know why I brought you here, new boy?" he asked, poking Maciii's head with his finger.

"No!" Maciii replied softly.

"About 20 minutes ago, I awoke feeling a little thirsty and when I feel thirsty there is only one solution…"

"Chocolate milk!"

"Don't join in, Snot. I put on my brown dressing gown and quietly slipped into my living quarters. Imagine my surprise, new boy!" and he poked J.B.'s head, "When I discovered every single piece of my prize chocolate furniture starting to melt! Every chocolate chair, every chocolate table, every highly prized chocolate ornament melting into a bubbling brown puddle of oozing goo!

Someone had been tampering with my air conditioning control and that someone was you!" he yelled, pointing an accusing finger at Maciii.

"We never went anywhere near your room!" Maciii quickly replied.

"You did, you did, you did! You broke into my room, hacked into Goldenbum and switched off the air.con. No one must tamper with Goldenbum. I need it for…" he paused and quickly looked at Gripe, "…my homework and essays and all sorts of school work!"

"We were asleep in bed. Honest!" said Maciii, holding up his hands innocently.

"Honest!" echoed J.B., holding up his hands innocently. Unfortunately his hands were covered in chocolate.

"Ha!" whooped Blowhole, moving his accusing finger from Maciii to J.B. "You have been caught brown–handed! See, Gripe, see! Chocolate-covered palms! What further evidence do you need of those naughty deed-doers' deeds?"

Sir Otto Gripe flopped into his desk chair and pondered quietly to himself. The clock on the bookshelf tick-tock-ticked to itself as he thought. Finally, he said, "But how do you know it's your chocolate, Blowhole?"

"Oh, for goodness sake! Snot, bring me that boy's hand!"

Snot grabbed J.B.'s chocolate-smeared hand, dragged it over to Blowhole with J.B. following and held it before his poky little eyes. Blowhole peered at it.

"Well, it looks like my chocolate!" Then he inhaled deeply. "It smells like my chocolate!" Then he unfurled his little villainous tongue and slowly ran it along J.B.'s palm.

"And it certainly tastes like my chocolate!"

"Gross!" said Maciii and Snot together.

Blowhole waggled J.B.'s choccy thumb in the head teacher's face. "Taste the chocolate!" Blowhole ordered.

"I really don't think I…"

"Taste the chocolate!"

"I don't think it's my place…"

"Taste the chocolate!"

Sir Otto reluctantly moved closer to the thumb, poked out his tiny teacher's tongue and gave it the swiftest of licks. Suddenly, his face lit up.

"Hmmm! Belgian chocolate. You know that tastes just like…"

"My furniture!" Blowhole finished his sentence for him.

"Your furniture," said Gripe, flopping back into his chair, "Yes, it does!"

Blowhole handed back J.B.'s hand and hissed softly, "This crime deserves the most severe punishment St Smugg's can offer…"

"You mean…?"

"Old Cranky!"

It turned out Old Cranky was an old, manky boat without sails, oars or much hope of ever sailing again. It sat on the golden beach between St Smugg's and what Blowhole described as "the most shark-infested ocean on the planet. Suckers!" Gathered around it was a group of solemn-faced children who had been summoned to the beach by the sombre dong of the school clock and stern wail of the school kazoo. Word had whizzed around the school of the naughty happenings the night before and each and every

51

child soon realised this was going to be a beach-bound assembly to remember.

Sir Otto was standing on a rickety podium next to Old Cranky, clutching his comfort hanky. Blowhole slunk back and forth surveying the crowd like a fox about to topple a wheelie bin.

As the final dong died away, Sir Otto coughed, blew his nose and addressed the children.

"Rarely in the history of St Smugg's has anyone committed a crime like the one we are to punish today! No one has ever been this naughty before!"

A mumble tumbled round the crowd. Pupils at St Smugg's committed crimes like this all the time; that's why they were there, and Sir Otto was the only one who knew nothing about it.

"And our new boys have been found guilty of breaking the one most precious rule of St Smugg's! And what is that rule?"

231 voices suddenly chanted,

"Don't get caught!"

"No, no, no. Don't do it in the first place. Bring forth the reprobates!"

To the slow beating of the school drum Maciii and J.B. were marched towards Old Cranky.

"What do you we do now?" whispered J.B.

"Well, excuse me, it wasn't me who got us into this sticky situation!"

J.B. sniggered, "Sticky! Like it!"

Maciii sighed his hundredth sigh of the morning as Snot lashed them to the deck of Old Cranky. Snot sniggered as he tied tight knots and hissed, "Usually Old Cranky bobs about a bit at sea then the punishees get rescued. Old tradition of a lesson teaching. Codswallop if you ask me. Only it seems Old Cranky's sprung a leak. Don't know how that happened. Old Cranky looks like it couldn't last more than half an hour in these waters. Seems to me you might be heading towards a watery grave!" He tied the final knot across J.B.'s wrists, sniffed and leapt off the boat.

"Wow!" nodded J.B. "What's codswallop?"

"Codswallop! Rubbish, garbage, not to be taken seriously!" Despite sounding like they should have come from Maciii's mouth these words came from a totally different mouth and it was very near J.B.'s ear.

"Clunk!"

"Squidgey!"

"What are you doing here?"

"I distracted Blowhole with a bit of chocolate and clambered aboard!"

"I mean it's lovely to see you and everything but I think we're about to be cast adrift in an old school tradition."

"This won't take long," she whispered, nudging past Maciii to get to J.B.

"Mind the other passenger!" groaned Maciii.

"Have you come to our rescue? Are you going to untie us? Are you going to set us free from the punishment?" asked J.B.

"No," said Clunk. "But Squidgey – I couldn't let you go without giving you this!"

And then she kissed him. A proper one. On the lips!

"This day can't get any worse!" moaned Maciii, averting

his gaze from the smoochy kiss to the seagulls circling above.

Clunk leapt overboard back onto the warm sand and disappeared in the throng of children awaiting the launch.

"What was all that about?" asked Maciii.

"Codswallop!" said J.B., dreamily.

And before Maciii could interrogate his partner any further they heard the words.

"Launch Old Cranky!"

And then there was a creaking, a squeaking, a growling, a howling and slowly, very slowly, Old Cranky started to slide towards the shark-infested sea.

Suddenly there was an almighty, ear-shocking splosh and droplets of fresh seawater spattered the faces of Maciii and J.B. Within seconds Old Cranky was bobbing on the ocean surface.

And if either of the boys had craned their necks ever so slightly and gazed down towards the end of the boat that Snot had been pointing at when he pointed out the hole in the deck, they might just have seen the first bubbling, trickle of fresh seawater as it sneakily leaked aboard the boat.

And they did and they saw and they screamed.

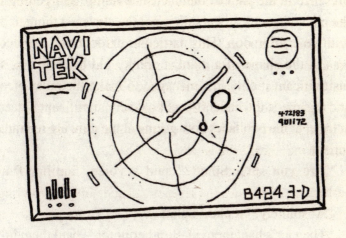

Chapter Six
"TOFFEE OVERBOARD!"

The Navi-Tek B424 3-D Modulating Radar aboard the British nuclear warship HMS Juggernautilus was blinking and bleeping a little more loudly and a little more urgently than it normally did. First Mate Colin Splatt had been trained at the best naval college in Britain so knew exactly where to hit it to stop it. The bleeping didn't stop so he hit it again, but the bleeping still bleeped on. So Colin Splatt scratched his beard and his bum, thought, tapped an emergency number into the Panaphonic K97 Blartophone then heard himself say the words, "Chief, I think we've found something!"

The bleeping on the radar indicated an unidentified

presence in the path of the nuclear warship, and getting in the path of a nuclear warship is not the cleverest thing to do with your afternoon. This particular unidentified presence was in the shape of a manky, cranky old boat. It was so insignificant it only just managed to make the radar bleep and this made the insignificant boat very significant indeed, at least, to the two faces now gazing at the glowing red radar screen.

"Are you sure, Splatt?" said a voice, familiar from earlier.

"Absolutely!" replied Splatt

"Then let's haul them in. Smitherington – haul them in!"

Old Cranky had been bobbing about for nearly three quarters of an hour by Maciii's calculation and in that time he'd counted 243 seagulls. J.B., who had counted far less, because counting seagulls, like counting sheep, made him sleepy, was gazing up at the sky.

"I wonder how they're going to rescue us?" he said, starting to feel the strain on his ties and keeping an eye on the increasingly deepening seawater around them.

"Any number of methods spring to mind. Helicopter…" Maciii suggested, still counting seagulls.

"I'd be v. miffed if it's the helicopter…"

"Raft, hydrofoil, dinghy, yacht, submarine…"

And at those words the boys suddenly heard a loud 'stonk', a strange 'clonk' and a worrying 'donk'. The boat suddenly stopped bobbing and J.B. noticed something.

"Why are the seagulls coming nearer?" asked J.B. as the confused expression of one bird drew unsettlingly close.

"They're not – we're getting closer to them!"

Then there was a huge sound of rushing, gushing water and the seagulls scattered out of the sky shrieking like cheap fireworks. The boys were, indeed, getting closer to the seagulls – well, the place recently vacated by the seagulls – and were rising higher and higher out of the water. The seawater, which had been thigh deep in the boat, was slowly draining out of the little seepy hole into which it had previously poured, and was now at least ankle deep and would very soon be only heel deep. J.B. and Maciii braced themselves for an onslaught of insults from Blowhole or some muttering admonishments from Gripe or some slavering needling from Snot, but what they actually heard was,

"Agents Maciii and J.B. – welcome back to MI3(and a bit)!"

Within several seconds six blue and white uniform-clad sailors were clambering across the tatty deck of Old Cranky slipping Maciii and J.B out of their knotted dilemma with ease. They smartly and swiftly saluted and leapt off again. But there was no splosh or splash as they disappeared. Maciii was the first to deduce what was happening and as he poked his face over the side of Old Cranky his suspicions were confirmed.

"We're on a submarine!" he yelped. "Triton T-class if I'm not mistaken!"

"No, you're not mistaken, Agent Maciii!" came the voice from the mouth just below the stern nose in the middle of the face of Colonel Cheese. "Triton T-class Nuclear Division, actually."

"How did you find us?" asked Maciii, leaping from Old Cranky closely followed by a slightly confused J.B. The Colonel said nothing and led them through the pokiest of portholes and deep into the claustrophobic hold of HMS Juggernautilus. Maciii wondered whether he should brief the Colonel about the recent goings-on. He decided not to and pressed a finger to his lip as J.B. nodded behind him and scratched his own lip thinking something was there.

An hour later Maciii and J.B. were sitting in front of two hot mugs of tea and two cold faces of their bosses, Cheese and Smitherington.

"So how did you find us?" asked Maciii, blowing on his tea.

"Yes, I was wondering that!" echoed J.B., who'd been wondering something entirely different.

"Give me your phone!" ordered Cheese, holding out her hand to J.B., who rummaged in his pocket then remembered what had happened the previous night.

"Here!"

Cheese quickly handed the phone to Smitherington who clicked it open and showed the boys the innards.

"GPS tracker," he explained, half to the boys and half to the Colonel. "You were being tracked throughout the mission by the MI3(and a bit) geostationary satellite which can locate this GPS tracker to anywhere on the planet within six millimetres. We identified you on the boat. Colonel Cheese gave the order, we rose out of the water and you were safely onboard the deck as we emerged! Simple!"

Maciii's whoop of laughter was quickly followed by J.B.'s. Suddenly, the mood in the room shifted from stern, formal military business to hearty friendship and gratitude. Colonel Cheese stretched her arms behind her head and said with a smile, "So tell us how you disabled Goldenbum!"

Maciii stopped whooping with laughter and fell silent. J.B. fell silent a little later – the mood in the room suddenly shifted back again

"Well?" asked Cheese, uncertainly, sitting up straight.

Maciii looked about for a moment trying to divert attention while he considered his answer. There was nothing for it but to confess.

"We didn't disable Goldenbum," Maciii said, softly.

"What?" Cheese barked, making Smitherington jump and slop his tea.

"He said 'We didn't disarm Goldenbum!'" repeated J.B. loudly, thinking Colonel Cheese was having difficulty hearing over the throbbing of the engines.

"You mean you haven't…after we…in this submarine…" She pointed a very pointy finger at Smitherington, "And you said…Ohhh!"

Colonel Cheese stomped from the room, stomped down the corridor – not easy to do in a very thin submarine corridor - stomped up the ladder and on the way up stomped her head against the porthole.

"Ouch!"

Smitherington wiped remnants of piping hot tea from his sleeve and said, "We were under the impression you had successfully completed the mission!"

Maciii and J.B. decided on their favourite response and just shrugged.

"Oh, come on, chaps! This is my job on the line here –

did you even make contact with Agent Samantha Clunk?"

"I made contact!" said J.B., imitating the splattering, smoochy kissing sound.

"Gross!" said Smitherington and Maciii together.

"Wait a minute," said Maciii stopping J.B. mid-smooch. "Did you say Agent Samantha Clunk?"

"Yes, Agent Clunk! She's been on MI3(and a bit)'s list for two years. You mean, she…" he pointed to the upper deck of the submarine where Colonel Cheese was currently stomping, "…didn't tell you about her…" he pointed in the general direction of St Smugg's.

Maciii and J.B. shook their heads in unison then shrugged again.

"Cripes, this is annoying! I mean, did Clunk give you any information? Did she give you anything at all?"

J.B. began, "She gave me…"

Maciii interrupted with, "We know what she gave you!"

But J.B. continued, "I was going to say she gave me this when she kissed me!"

And J.B. started poking about in his mouth whilst Maciii and the curious Smitherington gathered closer wondering what was about to emerge. J.B. poked a little deeper and then, with a slobbering squelch, a small silver-wrapped sweet came out. J.B. wiped it clean and offered it to Smitherington, who almost took it before saying, "Maciii, examine this, would you?"

Maciii reluctantly took it from J.B., wiped it again and held it up to the light.

"Seems like a boiled sweet, possibly a caramel. Standard silver wrapping available on the open market, but seems a little heavier than I would expect!"

He placed the silver-wrapped object on the desk and cautiously unwrapped it.

"OMG!" shouted Maciii, "OMG to the power of 1k!"

Smitherington and J.B. exchanged a glance, hoping one of them could explain the strange language Maciii was suddenly spouting. Neither could.

"LOL, LOL, LOL!" Maciii laughed out loud.

Another confused glance was exchanged. Maciii was whooping with laughter once again.

"Look at that!" and he picked about in the toffee and removed a small, silver disk about the size of a small coin from the wrapper and held it up. J.B. whooped loudly, clapped his hands in delight, did a little jig and then said, "I don't get it!"

"This is the Choc Chip!"

"I still don't get it!"

"I do!" Smitherington said suddenly, deadly serious, and swiped the Chip from Maciii's grasp. "The Choc Chip contains either single item of digitalised info about Goldenbum. We've been trying to get our hands on this for months. On this little chip is every item of info about how Blowhole plans to e-tweak chocolate to make it downloadable. This disc is worth millions…"

"Of sweets?" asked J.B.

"Of pounds!" Smitherington replied softly. And with that he was out of the door, stomping down the corridor, stomping up the ladder and stopping only to stomp his head on the porthole, "Ouch!", on to the deck of HMS Juggernautilus.

Colonel Cheese had stopped stomping and was quietly seething instead as Smitherington's head emerged from the porthole.

"We nearly had it in the palm of our hands, Smitherington!" she said, gazing out of the choppy, sloppy waters to St Smugg's Very Private School. "Just there!" She stabbed her palm to emphasise her point, and as she did, Smitherington slipped the Choc Chip into her held-out hand. There was a quiet moment as Colonel Cheese turned it over.

"Is this what I think it is, Smitherington?"

"What do you think it is, ma'am?"

Colonel Cheese checked no one was about. As they were miles from land no one was about, except for a couple of overconfident seagulls chattering to each other on the far side of the deck. Then she lowered her voice.

"Is this the Choc Chip?"

Smitherington nodded his head.

Colonel Cheese looked about again to make sure no one was still around and no one was still around, though the seagulls had hopped a little closer.

A smile wandered across Cheese's craggy face.

"Do you still have the phone?" she whispered. Smitherington bobbingly nodded once more and handed the GPS phone to his boss who pecked the tracker out of the phone and stuck it to the Choc Chip with glob of toffee.

"Now if it ever gets lost – we can locate it with the GPS tracker!"

"Brilliant, ma'am. Surely this calls for a promotion?"

"For me?"

"For me!"

Then they said, "For both of us!"

Cheese whooped a delighted whoop and tossed the Choc Chip playfully in the air and held out her hand to catch it again. Unfortunately, it didn't return.

"Seagull!" blared Smitherington, pointing at the cheeky gull who'd just swooped past Cheese in a flapping flurry of feathers and snatched the Choc Chip from the air. Colonel Cheese looked at her palm, then at the departing seagull, then at her palm again then at the departing seagull.

"Seagull!" she blared. "Find the seagull!"

"I don't think we can, ma'am!"

Cheese grabbed him by his dangling military tie and dragged his muttering face face to face with her face. And it wasn't a pretty face. Smitherington thought he could hear a sound like a boiling kettle.

"Find that flipping, flapping seagull, Smitherington, otherwise I'll break you down to third-class corporal quicker than you can say covert surveillance!"

Smitherington was about to say 'Covert surveillance?' but thought better of it. Cheese curled her lip to its curliest and snarled out her final order.

"Find the seagull!"

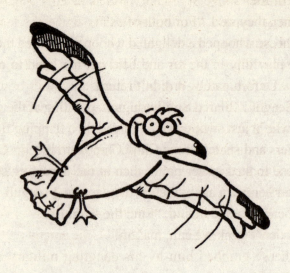

Chapter Seven
SEAGULL HUNT!

And when Colonel Cheese of MI3(and a bit) barked her most barkiest of orders, everyone jumped. Emails blazed across highly secure internet connections, phones calls chatted down scrambled lines, coded texts whizzed across continents and all with one simple message – 'Find the seagull!'

Across the country, engines roared into life, helicopters were leapt into like scalded toads, jump jets jumped higher than they'd ever jumped before, squadrons of black undercover cars swarmed through streets as if their lives depended on it and, if Colonel Cheese had anything to do with it (which she did), it would (and it did).

The skies above St Smugg's were suddenly clouded with scanning 'copters beaming spotlights across the land. The seagull must be somewhere!

Maciii slipped on his crash helmet and glanced over at J.B. who was struggling with his strap. Both boys were astride SK3/20 Kusuki jet-skis and both were quickly learning how to ride them.

"So that's the go-fast button?" asked J.B., bobbing on the water, struggling with his strap and trying not fall off all at the same time.

"No!" shouted Maciii, as he throttled up his own engine. "This is the go-fast button! The red is the emergency ejector seat!"

"Cool!"

"And this is the tracker radar. We're going to follow the seagull with that! Get it?"

"And that's the go-fast button?"

"YES!!"

J.B. throttled up his engine and it roared as loud as Maciii's.

"Cooler!"

Maciii held up his hand for a high-five. J.B. aimed at it as a huge wave whooshed him up and down; he slapped his knee and his face then hi-fived Maciii.

"First one to find the seagull gets a free lunch!" Maciii shouted and sped off across the waves.

"Coolest!" shouted J.B. and prodded a button on the jet-ski console. A TV advert shimmered into view advertising Downloadable ChocolateTM. J.B. stared lovingly at the choc for a few seconds before remembering he had something to do and then did it. He jabbed and stabbed a few random buttons on the console and the TV picture shivered away to be replaced by the bleeping, blinking screen of the Navi-Tek B424 3-D Modulating Radar, and something was bleeping on the blinking screen.

"Seagull!" J.B. roared at the screen then reversed the jet-ski, banged against the side of HMS Juggernautilus, pressed another button, lurched forward, banged against the side of HMS Juggernautilus again then pressed the go-fast button. The jet-ski whipped away across the frothy foaming waves with J.B. desperately clutching on.

J.B followed the bleeping signal which led him via a couple of bouncing buoys and an irate windsurfer towards the beach where he could see Maciii's jet-ski already grounded near some deckchairs. He flicked the go-fast button once again and sped bumpity-bump towards the beach. Then he tried to find the go-slow button. Then he remembered he hadn't asked which was the go-slow button. Perhaps it was the red one.

BANG!

"It's not the red one!" J.B. thought as he shot towards the clouds. He glanced down and saw the jet-ski, the beach and Maciii disappearing below his confused feet. Just as he reached the zenith of his trajectory, there was a moment's pause, and in that moment's pause a seagull casually flapped by which J.B. noticed had something silver and disc-like in its beak. His face lit up, and he pointed and yelled, "Seagull!", but by the time he'd got to the L of seagull he was on his way back down to earth wondering where his parachute was.

WHOOSH!

"It was the red button this time!" he smiled to himself as he floated beachwards under the safe canopy of his parachute, landed, scrabbled out and galloped towards Maciii.

"I've seen the seagull!" J.B. excitedly imparted to his impatient friend.

"Where?"

J.B. pointed upwards.

"That narrows it down a bit!" sighed Maciii. "Get on your bike!"

Two KT42 Vespas were leaning against an ice-cream van. Maciii gestured to J.B. to mount his and pointed at the buttons. "Go-fast! Go-slow!" He pointed at the road. "Go find the seagull!"

And with that very short driving lesson Maciii leapt aboard his Vespa, throttled up the engine, glanced at the Navi-Tek B424 3-D Modulating Radar on the handlebars and roared away leaving J.B. in a dusty cloud of fumes.

J.B. coughed, spluttered, muttered, wafted smoke then jumped aboard his Vespa and sped off in the completely opposite direction to Maciii.

And while Maciii and J.B. and the covert military power of MI3(and a bit) were scouting about to find a seagull, something was consuming the attention of the rest of the planet. Over the last few hours adverts for Downloadable ChocolateTM had been cropping up and popping up all over the globe. Twitface.com was suddenly flooded with trailers, snippets, outtakes, home movies and bloopers all connected with Downloadable ChocolateTM. Sox News

Corporation (sponsored by Downloadable ChocolateTM) was hourly reporting on the world's strange and unexplained interest in Downloadable ChocolateTM. Sport events across the world halted as their intervals were longer than the games and every single interval was filled with adverts for Downloadable ChocolateTM.

Every newspaper, magazine, comic, swap card pack, T-shirt, baseball cap, candy wrapper, TV show, was covered with adverts for Blowhole's Downloadable ChocolateTM.

And somewhere deep in the darkest room of St Smugg's a crackling, cackling laugh was rattling round the corridors.

Meanwhile, halfway down the pet food aisle of a Supafresh supermarket, J.B. realised he was still riding his Vespa. He realised this because a thuggish, thick voice suddenly said, "You can't ride that Vespa in here!"

The thick, thuggish voice belonged to the thick, thuggish face of a stocky security guard who glared down at J.B. as if he'd just said something rude about his sister. He growled, "Get off it now!" and pointed at his 'Happy to Help' badge.

"But I'm bleeping!" explained J.B., pointing to the Navi-Tek B424 3-D Modulating Radar on his handlebars. The Happy to Help security guard was happy to help J.B. off the Vespa with his happy to help fists. He tumbled into a moaning heap near the cat litter and groaned as he saw the security guard wheeling the Vespa out of the supermarket and into a skip. He gathered his thoughts – which for J.B. took a little longer than most people – and stood up. It was then he heard the bleeping. In the struggle the Navi-Tek B424 3-D Modulating Radar had snapped off the handlebars and was still bleeping merrily to itself on the floor. J.B. swiftly scooped it up and gazed at it. The bleeping spot was indicating a nearby location and J.B was determined to locate it. He strode off down the aisle, turned left, turned right, turned right again then stood exactly where the radar had guided him – the fish counter.

"Good morning, sir. Could I interest you in a halibut?" said a jolly fishmonger from beneath his straw hat. His eyebrows were as thick as his moustache and his eyes as wide as his fish's.

"I want a seagull!" explained J.B., which didn't explain a lot.

The jolly fishmonger waved a hand across the fine array of fish and said, "Could I interest you in a crab, perhaps?"

The fishmonger had had a lot of strange requests in his fishmongering years but no one had ever asked for seagull.

"Sea-gull!" J.B. thought if he said it slower it would make more sense. It didn't.

"Shrimp, perhaps, sir?"

The bleeping on the Navi-Tek B424 3-D Modulating Radar was bleeping more loudly and incessantly than J.B. had ever heard it bleep before. He waved it over the crowd of fishy faces.

"Self-scanning, eh, sir?"

As he held the Navi-Tek B424 3-D Modulating Radar over a squid the bleeper bleeped its bleepiest and J.B. heard himself saying, "I'll have that squid, please!"

Unfortunately a nanosecond before J.B. had said, "I'll have that squid, please!" a woman in a pink hat to his right had said, "I'll have that squid, please!"

And the eager fishmonger had slapped the squid on the counter, wrapped it, bagged it, labelled it and handed it to the woman with a jolly, "Happy to help!"

Before J.B. had taken in what was happening the woman was half way down the aisle with her catch under her arm and J.B. close behind.

"Give me the squid!" he demanded, skipping alongside, forgetting his manners.

"What?" said the bewildered woman under her pink hat, gathering her coat lapels closer.

"Give…me…the…squid!" repeated J.B., thinking if he said it louder it would make more sense. It didn't.

"Get your own squid. This is my squid!" said the woman, dodging a stand advertising Downloadable ChocolateTM as she headed for the checkout.

"I want the squid! That squid!" J.B. jabbed the bag, causing the woman to shriek to the stocky happy to help security guard who cracked his knuckles by the self-scan counter.

"I'm bleeping!" J.B. thought if he showed the woman the Navi-Tek B424 3-D Modulating Radar it might help. It didn't. The woman swiftly scanned the squid, swiped her card and made for the door. J.B. was about to make after her when he felt a stocky fist on his shoulder shoving him against the self-scan counter.

"Unexpected item in the bagging area!" said the machine, brightly.

"You don't go around prodding people's purchases in Supafresh!" snarled the guard. "Now scram!" And so J.B. scrammed.

Out on the Supafresh car park a spattering of rain was splattering the tarmac and J.B. kicked a little litter bin in frustration. It was then he saw the pink-hatted lady getting into a yellow taxi. What could he do? He glanced over at the trolley park where a gaggle of metal shopping trolleys were clustered, unwanted and unused. It was then J.B. put two and two together and as usual the answer wasn't four.

Two and half miles away from Supafresh the pink-hatted lady relaxed, stretched her legs and gazed out at the flashing shops as they zapped past.

Tap-tap-tap!

A sale at Pacy's!

Tap-tap-tap!

Another of those adverts for Downloadable ChocolateTM!

Tap-tap-tap!

Half-price lemons at Malloy's!

Tap-tap-tap!

Whatever is that tap-tap-tapping, thought the pink-hatted lady turning to see where it was coming from. And when she saw where it was coming from her eyebrows did a hundred somersaults. It was coming from J.B. and he was sitting in a jiggering, juddering, bumpity-bumping shopping trolley and clutching onto the back bumper of the taxi for his dear life. The pink-hatted lady rubbed her eyes as she stared at the bizarre sight. She rubbed her nose and ears too, but it wouldn't go away. She peered closer and could swear J.B. was mouthing the word, "Squid!"

The woman shrieked an order at the cab driver who screeched the cab to a halt. J.B.'s trolley slammed crash-bang into the rear of the cab and sent its occupant sprawling and howling through the air, smashing through a door and slap crash-bang onto the luxuriously carpeted floor of a very posh restaurant.

J.B. moaned, groaned, moaned again to make sure he still could and rolled over onto his back. He fluttered his eyes and tried to focus on the face gazing down at him. The figure was silhouetted against the light but the voice was one J.B immediately recognised, "Ah, J.B.! I've been expecting you!"

Chapter Eight
"NEVER TAKE SWEETIS OFF STRANGERS!"

"Sodium Walproate Empilium Endogenous Trivarium Indocarm Soloonium! Otherwise known as SWEETIS – one of the strongest sedatives on the planet. People clonk out within milliseconds of taking it – that's why you should never take SWEETIS off strangers!"

Two crackling, cackling laughs echoed around J.B.'s fuzzy, wuzzy head waking him to consciousness. He tried to speak but all he managed was

"Blarrhhhhhhhhh!"

He tried again.

"Blarrrrrhhh!"

"Wipe his chin, Snot, he's dribbling!" The face of the nasal-inverted servant approached J.B.'s focus-zone like a hedgehog trotting up to a bowl of milk. He produced a brown handkerchief, spat on it and wiped J.B.'s face.

"Blllllaaaaarrrhhhhhhhhhhhh!!"

Second by second more images flooded into sharper focus and J.B. slowly began to remember what had happened a few hours earlier. Whilst lying sprawled out on the luxurious carpet of the restaurant (after he had been catapulted from a super market trolley (after he had chased the pink-hatted lady from the supermarket)) a mysterious stranger had approached him and said (in a rather OTT way, thought J.B.), "Ah, J.B.! I've been expecting you!" and offered him a chocolate which the bewildered J.B. noddingly accepted. Within milliseconds he had clonked out completely.

"Blaaaaarrrrhh!" J.B. tried to articulate something again but failed again.

"You are now in my hands!" J.B. recognised the slithering voice of Oleg Blowhole and, as he squinted his eyes, he recognised the slithering face of Oleg Blowhole too. He didn't like either.

"Blllaaaaaarrhhh!" J.B. tried for a fifth time.

"It'll wear off. In the meantime I have some ranting to do. Snot, is my tie straight?"

"Yes, sir!"

J.B. could make out the chocolate-brown suited little figure as he marched up and down and back again nibbling on a chocolate bar.

"Firstly, welcome to my father's chocolate restaurant.

He died a horrible death and left it all to me. No one knows how he died. Well, perhaps someone does." Blowhole winked at himself in a nearby mirror. "I really must apologise for tying you to a chair. It seemed the wisest policy!"

Blowhole stamped his foot to emphasise his point.

"Owwww!" yelled Snot.

"Well, don't stand so close!" hissed Blowhole, and snapped off another bit of chocolate. "Normally I would use rope or duct tape for such a procedure but my ever-helpful servant couldn't find any, buy any, steal any or even get any off Freebay. So you are tied to the chair with a rope woven to twice the strength of any industrial cable and made entirely from chocolate wrappers!"

J.B.'s bleary eyes followed Blowhole as he strutted around like the proudest of peacocks, tossing chocolate wrappers over his shoulder. Suddenly he turned, strutted over to J.B. and froze him with his piercing 'don't mess with me' glare.

"Do you think I'm an idiot?" he roared, splattering relics of semi-chewed choc in J.B's face. "Do you think I'm a complete moron! Do I look stupid?"

J.B. wanted to answer "Yes" to all three questions but all he could manage was,

"Blarrrhhh!"

"Of course I knew where the Choc Chip was all the time, didn't I, Snot?"

Snot was inspecting his bruised and unsocked foot, but managed an agreeing grunt.

"How could I control the most ambitious industrial

scheme ever conceived without knowing where my Choc Chip was? You see, we at Blowhole EnterprisesTM, have a tracking device too. Snot, waggle our tracking device in his face!"

Snot sighed, wondered whether to put his sock back on, wondered against it and slipped a little bleeping, blinking black device from his jacket pocket and waggled it.

"See! Am I stupid now?"

"Blarhhh!"

"So as you were shooting here and there on your little jet-ski and motorbikes we were sitting snugly here tracking the entire progress. What you don't know, though, is what we know. Do you want to know what we know that you don't know?"

J.B. tried to nod his head but the last traces of the drug were making it go all wobbly.

"I'm thinking that's a nod, sir!"

Blowhole hissed, "The seagull dropped the Choc Chip! I saw it all on CCTV; it plopped into the water and was swallowed by a small squid. That squid!"

And Blowhole pointed triumphantly at a small plastic bag which a few hours earlier J.B. had been prodding.

"The squid was netted by Supafresh fishermen and deposited on the fish counter within minutes of being caught and was bought by Norma Stump!"

Blowhole pointed triumphantly in the opposite direction as the pink-hatted lady suddenly emerged from the shadows and waved.

"She works for me. J.B., this is Norma Stump. Norma Stump, this is J.B. I had her bring me the squid and lure you here all at the same time! How clever am I?"

"Blarrhhh!"

Blowhole wafted Stump away and she disappeared back into the shadows, then he flopped into a chair and bridged his fingers, tapping the tips over and over again. He poked a chocolate button on the desk and a distant buzzer buzzed.

"Yes, sir?" said Snot, who'd resocked his foot and was standing in it next to his boss.

"I'm not buzzing you, I'm buzzing Dwayne Deek. They're two completely different buzzes!" He buzzed another buzzer to demonstrate his point and both sounded exactly the same.

"Oh, yes, sir, sorry, sir!" said Snot reversing into Dwayne Deek who'd just entered the room. Deek, who was dressed in a glimming white lab coat with a pocket stuffed with pens, snorted the geekiest of snorts, mumbled an apology then peered through his thick glasses until he spotted his boss.

"Blowhole, I need that information! There's no way I can e-tweak the molecular structure of chocolate without the files off the Choc Chip! And the deadline is approaching fast!"

Blowhole beamed a sinister smile in Deek's direction silencing him. The uber-geek scanned the room and saw the bleary eyed J.B. dribbling in the corner.

"That's J.B.! From St Smugg's!" said Deek, snatching his glasses from his inquisitive face and cleaning them. "What's he doing here?"

Blowhole tap-tap-tapped his fingertips and slowly said, "He brought you a present!"

"Wow! Where is it?"

"In that squid!" Blowhole triumphantly pointed.

Deek looked at Snot who shrugged, he then looked at Blowhole who smirked, he then looked at J.B. who dribbled. Blowhole raised his eyebrows and nodded in the direction of the squid. And when Oleg Blowhole raised his eyebrows and nodded in the direction of anywhere then that's exactly where you should go. Deek went. He cautiously leaned over the bag, cautiously opened it and even more cautiously slipped in his hand. As he rummaged around there was a squelching, belching, rubbery, blubbering sound and a couple of odd burpy noises too. Deek wasn't enjoying his present much until his inquisitive fingers wrapped around a shape he recognised. A hard, plastic Choc Chippy shape!

"The Choc Chip!" yelled Deek, whipping it from the squid together with a handful of oozy goo which flew through the air.

"Ugh!" said Snot, touching his face.

"Take the Chip to the Factory, download all the relevant files and set the process in motion! Now!"

Deek nodded eagerly, smiled, smirked, wiped his hands on his trousers and fled from the room.

A silence hung in the air as the door slammed shut. A clock ticked, Snot hummed and J.B. said,

"What are you…blarrhhhh?"

"Ah, at last, articulate words. I told you it'd wear off eventually. What am I going to do with the Choc Chip? Well, allow me to explain." And he grabbed a chocolate bar and leapt to his cocky feet. "Downloadable ChocolateTM is without doubt the most important candy initiative in the history of world confectionery. You will have no doubt seen the aggressive marketing campaign which has ensured every single person on the planet will know about Downloadable ChocolateTM and more importantly everyone will want it! Launch date is Saturday 1200 GMT, 1300 CET, 1700 EST. We have estimated a download projection of 1,000,000,000 hits within the first hour of trading. And I, together with my affiliates in territories throughout the globe, will be millionaires by the end of the day. And happy little children throughout the world will have their Downloadable ChocolateTM. It's foolproof!"

J.B. knew he was lying but could only dribble and say, "Why…are…you…telling…?"

"Why am I telling you this? Because the next thing to happen in your scrawny little life will render you completely speechless. It is time for your punishment! Snot, prepare the gerbils!"

Twenty minutes later J.B.'s blurry eyes were staring down at his sockless feet dangling below him, each coated with gooey, oozy cheese sauce. He stared, confused as the sauce drip-drip-dripped away. Below his dangling, cheesy feet was a large, rusty old mixing bowl about the size of a garden swimming pool, with strange scratching-scraping sounds coming from under its cover. He couldn't help wondering why.

"This is a 1929 Shermshey Y-79 Influx Agitating Mixer!" Blowhole's boast rang out, and bounced around the room as he stood stroking the bowl. "My father designed it as the first mixing bowl in the world to handle three hundred thousand litres of melted top-quality chocolate. It hasn't been used for over seventy years! Until today! Snot, you know what to do!"

Snot did know what to do, but he didn't want to do it. He'd already mutteringly dragged J.B.'s limp body up the ladder and sweatingly, gruntingly wrapped him to the dangling arm hanging over it. He'd then leaned back on a railing, blown his nose, wiped his forehead and then, even more reluctantly than before, turned to a dusty panel of levers and pulleys. On Blowhole's order he grunted and slapped a button. The ageing mechanics juddered into loud life.

Budder, budder, budder!

Blowhole was shouting something probably very sinister and undoubtedly sarcastic, but his words were buddered away by the judder of the machine. Realising he was wasting his time Blowhole thumbed the air impatiently and Snot soon got the message. He very slowly pulled another cranking lever and J.B soon noticed he was not the only one dangling over the bowl. Another crane arm had gradually and squeakingly swung out. Hanging from it was someone dressed in pink feathers, pink dress and a slightly battered pink hat.

"Samantha!" cried J.B., more than a little bemused and bewildered. "What are you…? I mean, how did…? When…? What did…?" But all his words were swamped by the thundering budder, budder, budder.

Down on the dry, cementy floor Blowhole was mouthing words as expressively as his little mouth would let him. But they too were lost in the buddering. He rolled his eyes upwards, downwards and a couple of time sidewards then made a throat cutting action at Snot who ceased the buddering with a sharp slap of a button. The machine juddered into silent stillness until all that could be heard was the creaking, squeaking swinging of the two crane arms.

"Samantha! How lovely to see you again," said J.B. "Do forgive me for not shaking hands!"

Clunk shrugged.

"So polite, J.B.!" rasped Blowhole from below. "So very, very polite. Now you may be wondering why Miss Clunk is joining you!"

Samantha squeaked behind her gag and shrugged a lot.

"Miss Clunk is probably wondering why she is joining you too! You see, Miss Clunk, whom I once treated as a close friend and ally, has been caught with her fingers in the cookie jar. Haven't you, Miss Clunk?"

Samantha squeaked and shrugged and tried a bit of wriggling, but none of it worked.

"Show the pictures, Snot!"

Snot rummaged under his sweaty armpit and whipped out a wodge of photographs which he wafted in the direction of the two confused and increasingly frightened faces.

"Can you see what these photographs show?"

Both J.B. and Clunk shook their heads.

"Erm…Snot, describe the pictures."

Snot pulled his 'do-I-have-to-do-everything-face' and then muttered, "Ermm…dark room…erm…Mr. Blowhole's quarters…erm…shadowy figure…possibly Miss Clunk!"

Blowhole coughed a sneering cough that echoed round the room.

"Definitely Miss Clunk…and on this one she's opening Mr Blowhole's desk drawer…erm…and on this one, oh, look at that…she's putting her little hand in the drawer…and this one…she's taking something out of the drawer…looks like it might be….

Cough, cough, echo, echo.

"It is…. The Choc Chip! She stole the Choc Chip. Naughty! And this one is…erm…this is Mr Blowhole on a donkey at the seaside…with his little sun hat on…and this one…!"

"That's enough, Snot! Put them away!"

Snot put them away. Blowhole's beady eyes suddenly blazed like he'd eaten too many E-numbers and he bellowed, "Stolen! Stolen! You had the nerve to steal my Choc Chip and then (and then!) you had the nerve to pass it onto him!" He jabbed the air with a pointed finger at J.B. "You passed it to him – when you kissed him! You hid it in the side of your mouth and slipped it into his when you kissed. That is so gross!"

J.B. and Clunk blushed.

"And when people do things like that to me – I do things like this to them! Snot, uncover the bowl!"

And with the slap of another button the cover of the giant mixing bowl slowly slid away revealing something which made Clunk stare in horror, J.B. scowl in slight confusion and Snot and Blowhole giggle in malicious glee. In the mixing bowl were two hundred gingerish gerbils scurrying and hurrying and banging and bumping against each other.

"Norwegian gerbils, starved for fourteen days and trained to nibble anything cheesy!" announced Blowhole. "Their incisor teeth have been sharpened daily until they have become like razors. Teeth like razors!" He said it again because he liked the echo. He sneered up at J.B. and Clunk, helplessly and hopelessly bound and dangled, and slowly slipped a small chunk of cheese from his pocket.

"Edam!" he said, casually sniffing it and then just as casually tossed it into the bowl. Mayhem broke out. The squealing was ear shattering as gerbil after gerbil kicked and scratched and nibbled towards the small bit of cheese. Gerbil clambered over gerbil, gerbil sneaked under gerbil. They were all elbowing their way to the only morsel of food they had sniffed in days.

"Peckish!" said Blowhole, approvingly. "They love their cheese. That's why I've had your naked toes coated in cheese sauce!" He winked a vicious wink and said very slowly, "Snot! Lower…" But before he could complete the sentence with the word, "Away" he stopped, narrowed his eyes and then cupped his ear.

"Is that somebody's phone?"

Faintly but clearly above the noise of the ravenous gerbils could be heard the distinct bleep-bleep-bleep of an incoming text.

Snot looked about then pointed accusingly at J.B.

"Give!" And Snot stretched his little body as far has he could over the bowl towards the dangling victim and rummaged in his pocket. Chewing gum, string, a comb, some hair gel and finally a bleeping, vibrating phone. He tossed it down to Blowhole who deftly caught it and stared at the screen.

How R U? whr R U m8?

"Oh, it's from your little friend, Maciii. Isn't that nice? He's concerned about you!" Then Blowhole's face changed as a malevolent thought scuttled through his mind. He cackled to himself and started tapping into the phone.

K, m8. MEt me @ d chocl@ rstRNt uz GPS 2 fnd TH8 9HZ

And then he jabbed 'Send', cackled, cackled some more and smacked his lips.

"I think we're going to have a visitor!"

And a few miles away Maciii's phone bleeped with the incoming message. He read it, whispered, "Cool!", tapped the postcode into his e-phone then kick-started his Vespa.

Chapter Nine
SACKED!

On top of the Chocolate Restaurant Oleg Blowhole was peering at Maciii's beetling progress in the street below like a hungry raven about to swoop. His jelly bean eyes snooped through the D39-K2 Duo Prismatic Binoculars on every swerve of Maciii's Vespa.

"Soon you, too, will be ensnared in my scheme, entangled by my brilliance and nibbled by my gerbils – keep going, Maciii, keep going!"

He tip-tapped the last five words into J.B.'s phone and bleeped it over to Maciii who skidded to a halt, read the message and then redoubled his efforts. Blowhole slipped his own phone from his pocket, punched a key and held it to his evil ear.

"Hello, Snot?…it's me…what do you mean 'who?'…who do you think it is? Alright, who do I sound like?…no, I do not! She's got a lisp! It's Blowhole…OLEG Blowhole! Don't salute the phone, Snot. Listen. Are you listening, Snot? OLEG BLOWHOLE! Your boss! Are you holding the phone the right way up? Listen, our target is approaching. Be at the corner of…"

He peered once more into the D39-K2 Duo Prismatic Binoculars to check the sign on the street corner to which Maciii was headed. "…Mackilliguddie Street and Macguddikillie Street in two minutes time." Blowhole sighed and repeated, "It's perfectly simple. Be at the corner of Mackillguddie Street and Macguddiekillie Street in two minutes time. Do I have to repeat everything? I said, do I have to repeat everything?" Blowhole snatched the phone from his ear and waggled a warning finger at it, realised what he was doing, quickly looked about to see no one had witnessed his waggling and put the phone back to his ear. "Get a big sack or something. As soon as Maciii goes past on his Vespa – bag him! Bag him in the sack!"

He snapped the phone shut and continued peering at his prey as Maciii grew closer. Suddenly, Blowhole's view was obliterated. For a fleeting moment he was confused. He slapped the binoculars and tried to refocus, recalibrate and rejigg, but something was still blocking his view. Something very large. He swiftly adjusted a few dials and zoomed out.

Within a nanosecond the words 'Downloadable ChocolateTM – coming to a store near you soon!' came into focus in bright dayglo red and green colours.

"How ironic! Blocked from seeing my target by one of my own advertisements!" Blowhole hissed. "Be patient, Oleg!" Blowhole waited a few short seconds and was about to call and have the driver fired when the Vespa popped out from behind the truck put-put-putting as before.

"Perfect!" The word slithered slowly from Blowhole's mouth as he panned the binoculars to the end of the street. He could just about make out Snot crouching uncomfortably behind a garbage skip clutching a large unmanageable sack. From his position Blowhole had the perfect vantage point to view the events that were about to unfold in the next few minutes. He sniggered, he snickered, he giggled, he even managed a small gurgle as every part of his complex plan began snapping into place. Perhaps he should give himself some kind of award, he thought, a medal for services to chocolate?

The Vespa put-put-putted towards the corner of Mackilliguddie Street and Macguddikillie Street within twenty metres of Snot. Snot was trembling.

Ten metres! Snot was still trembling.

Five metres! Tremble, tremble.

One metre! Snot clutched his sack to his chin, took a deep breath, whooped like a surprised whelk, leapt like a tubby elk and with one swift scoop swallowed up the figure on the Vespa. The bike put-put-putted out of control, wiggled, waggled and crashed into some bins. Snot tied the wriggling sack with some rough cord and slung it (still wriggling) over his shoulder. He spun triumphantly, thumbs-upped his boss on the other end of the binoculars and scurried away.

On top of the Chocolate Restaurant Blowhole thumbs-upped back, gave a little yelp of delight and trip-trapped down the rusty steps and back inside.

Minutes later Blowhole was pointing at a spot near his fireplace and hissing, "Plonk it there!" Snot plonked.

The glittering fire lit up Blowhole's face and crackled as he cackled, "So, welcome to my inner sanctum. You may have thought you had me in the palm of your hand; now I have you in mine!" He showed the palm of his hand but realised it couldn't be seen. "You thought you could tangle with Oleg Blowhole and disrupt one of the finest criminal schemes in the history of candy. Well, you were wrong, very wrong! Snot, remove the sack!"

Snot's stumbling thumbs untangled the knot and threw back the sack. The sweating head it revealed smiled nervously. Blowhole's face collapsed into quivering confusion, his eyes squinted and unsquinted as he tried to work out what he was looking at.

"Who the heck are you? And what are you doing in my sack?" he finally said.

"Captain Smitherington MI3(and a bit)!" said Captain Smitherington of MI3 (and a bit), smiling proudly and sweating profusely.

Blowhole seethed, wondered what to do, couldn't think of anything so seethed some more. "But…you… where…when…how?" His eyes fell on Snot whose eyes had fallen on his fingernails. "Snot!"

"Sir?"

"Slap yourself!" Snot slapped himself. "Now slap him!"

Smitherington held up a defensive hand. "You can't slap me, I'm property of Her Majesty!" he explained.

"Snot, slap yourself again, then!" and Snot slapped himself again, then.

The logs in the fireplace snapped and the flames twinkled and winked. Blowhole paced some more and nibbled a fingernail.

"However did you get in the sack?" he snarled at Smitherington, who gazed up at the ceiling saying, "I can't tell you that, sir, top secret!"

"Tell me or I'll roughly pluck the hairs from your nose!"

"That's property of Her Majesty, too, sir!"

Blowhole pulled a glinting and vicious-looking pair of tweezers from his pocket and snapped them threateningly before Smitherington's startled face.

"Maciii was pedalling down the street. I was dressed as him hidden behind one of those big advertising trucks. Soon as he arrived I leapt on and took over the journey. Then he jumped out and bagged me in the sack. Simple!" He added.

The flames reflected in Blowhole's eyes as he tapped his glistening lips and whispered, "So where is Maciii?"

"Can you hear something squeaking, Sammy?" asked J.B. as he gazed down at the razor-sharp gerbil teeth chattering below them. Samantha's gagged mouth made her reply unintelligible. She might have been saying, "No!" or "Don't call me Sammy!" or "You know very well I can't reply because I have this huge gag over my mouth!" Whichever way, J.B. smiled as he swung past her for the umpteenth time.

"You know, you kind of get used to this after a while. Quite comfortable in a funny sort of way."

Samantha's reply was, "Humf-um-umf-ggrr-ooop!" and, had she not been gagged, J.B. would have heard, "Look, you doofus, there's a dirty great big climbing rope just dropped down from the roof and I think someone is climbing down it!", but she was so he didn't. The newly dangled climbing rope flopped in front of Samantha's face and she grunted and huffed trying to draw J.B.'s attention to it. It wasn't an easy job.

"I could hang here all day if they let me, you know!"

As he swung past Samantha for the umpteenth and first time, she kicked him soundly in the shin.

"Ouch! Stop it!" He swivelled as best he could to look at Samantha and then looked at what she was looking at.

"I say, there's a dirty great big climbing rope just come down from the roof and I think someone is climbing down it!"

Samantha made a noise which, if it could be translated, couldn't be published. Both pairs of eyes peered into the roofy darkness above and very slowly a pair of training shoes appeared – training shoes J.B. recognised. These were quickly followed by a familiar pair of jeans, a very familiar T-shirt and all three were followed by a familiar head.

"Maciii!" shouted J.B.

"Mmmmmekkeeee!" muffled Samantha.

"Shhh!" hushed Maciii, then smiled. "Impressive, huh? Played a Double-Back-Swap-Ploy on Blowhole using Smitherington! Left me free to rescue you!"

"Wow, the Double-Back-Swap-Ploy!" said J.B. He was

about to say, "That's my favourite ploy!" but was interrupted by Samantha saying, "HHmmuff-huff-huff-ummmfff!" which, when Maciii ripped off her gag, came out as, "Will you two dorks stop talking and get us out of here?"

Maciii grasped his rope nervously and started to swing. Building up more and more momentum, he swung back and forth a few times then, convinced he'd built up enough force, grabbed Samantha and pushed her over to the platform where Snot had once stood. She tottered slightly, but then found her balance and leaned against the handrail. Maciii pushed off again and grabbed hold of J.B. pulling him back towards the platform. He touched his toes on the rusty surface but couldn't grip. The two swung back over the bowl and Maciii kicked against the far side sending them swinging safely back onto the platform. Maciii sighed with relief, wiped his brow and unclipped himself from his climbing rope.

"Well done!" hooted J.B. "High-five? Oh, no, we're still tied up!"

But Maciii was ahead of J.B, as he always was, and he leaned down into the chattering swarm of evil-toothed gerbils. Samantha shouted, "Be careful!" But within seconds Maciii was holding a snarling, though slightly confused, gerbil in his hands.

"Don't point that gerbil at me!" said J.B.

Maciii winked, dropped to his knees, and whilst holding the gerbil in one hand ran his finger along the cheesy goo on their feet. He then swiftly transferred the goo to the paper wrapping them both and very carefully held the gerbil towards it. Within seconds the vicious incisors of the ravenous gerbil had nibbled, gnawed and gnarled their way through the wrappers freeing J.B. and Samantha. Maciii winked and released the gerbil back into the mixing bowl causing chaos amongst the rest of the swarm who clambered all over each other trying to lick his lips.

"How impressive was that?" Maciii smirked.

"Very. Now can we, please, get out of here?" demanded Samantha, and they started hurrying down the squeaking, creaking steps.

Suddenly, Maciii's mobile trilled into life giving off an ear-piercing ringtone which everyone except Maciii hated.

"Whatever is that?" shouted J.B.

"My new ringtone. Cool, yeah?"

"Not that, that!" Both Samantha and Maciii stopped their hurrying getaway and turned to where J.B. was pointing his inquisitive finger. He was pointing it at two hundred gerbil heads peering out of the giant bowl towards them. Or, more accurately, towards Maciii's mobile. As he moved it back and forth two hundred gerbil heads moved back and forth with it. Wherever the mobile went their eyes followed.

"It's the ringtone. They're responding to the ringtone. Look!" He ran up and down past their hypnotised faces and each and every face followed the mobile, leaning forward to get closer.

Maciii stopped and all the faces stopped and stared.

"I've got a plan!" said Maciii, softly but firmly. He jabbed a key silencing the ringtone and the gerbils sighed and flopped back into the bowl.

"What is it?"

"You'll see – all you have to do is release the gerbils."

"Did he just say release the gerbils?" Samantha asked J.B., who shrugged.

"Okay, put on those builders' boots first so they don't smell the cheese – then release the gerbils!"

J.B. shrugged again and started doing what he was asked whilst Samantha stood by trying to make sense of what was happening.

"What are you doing now?"

"Calling J.B.'s mobile!"

It was answered by the snarling, snide voice of Blowhole.

"I just tried to call you! Where are you, you snivelling brat?"

"It's okay. It's okay. We give in."

J.B. and Samantha snapped around when they heard Maciii's words.

"You give in?"

"Yes, we're coming up now to surrender. You were too good for us, Blowhole. We give in!"

"I knew you'd see sense. Good plan!"

"Good plan!" repeated J.B. as the gerbils swarmed around his feet. Maciii hung up and starting punching more keys.

"What are you doing?" asked Samantha.

"Sending my ringtone to J.B.'s phone!" explained Maciii.

"Good plan!" nodded J.B.

"Am I the only one wondering which part of this plan is the good part?" asked Samantha as she followed Maciii and

93

J.B towards Blowhole's office. But then Maciii began explaining his plan.

A sneering leer rippled across Oleg Blowhole's glistening lips and his smug, black eyebrows danced with glee as he clapped his hands three times with great pomp. He waited, then clapped them again with slightly less pomp. He waited, then hissed.

"Go and let them in, Snot!"

Snot swung open the big brown doors up ahead and three figures slowly sloped in with their hands held in the air looking very sad and downcast, perhaps a little too sad and downcast. Blowhole couldn't resist a taunt.

"So, you couldn't take it anymore? You gave in? You realised I was the superior intellect? You wimped out?"

They all noddingly agreed.

"Yep, all those things. Gave in...superior intellect...wimped out!" Said Maciii.

Blowhole began pacing before them, relishing every stride.

"Good, good, good. I'm very pleased. Now I must conjure up some devious and devilish punishment! Something toe-curlingly vile, something ear-achingly painful, something bum-wipingly..."

"Sorry, to interrupt..." interrupted J.B., "But Samantha would like to say something!"

"Oh, yes, I want to say, Maciii wants to say something!" said Samantha.

"Well, one of you say it and say it soon!"

Maciii pulled out his mobile and flipped the lid. "I just

wanted to make one last phone call!" And he jabbed a key.

"Snot, stop him!"

Snot lurched over as quickly as Snot could lurch, which wasn't very quickly, wondering how he could stop Maciii doing something he was already doing. But it was too late. J.B.'s phone, which was sat snugly in Blowhole's pocket, burst into trilling life.

"Whatever is that hideous noise?" screeched Blowhole, holding his hands over his ears.

Snot mouthed the word "phone!"

"What are trying to say?" shouted Blowhole, over the piercing trill.

Snot mouthed the word "phone!" but with an even bigger mouth this time.

"Speak up, you doofus!" shouted Blowhole.

Snot sighed the deepest of sighs, strode back to his boss, fished the phone from his pocket and jabbed off the ringtone.

He was about to loudly and clearly say the word "phone" but instead heard himself loudly and clearly saying the word, "Gerbil!" At that moment a small, malicious-looking, gerbil had appeared on the sideboard next to Blowhole. The knife-sharp incisors snippity-snapped together like an evil stapler. The gerbil's eyes gleamed at Blowhole.

"One little gerbil doesn't scare me!" announced Blowhole, and at those words the other one hundred and ninety-nine gerbils tumbled into the room and surrounded them both.

"Snot, do something!" ordered Blowhole.

"I am doing something."

"What are you doing?"

"I'm starting to cry, sir!"

Snot suddenly hugged his boss. Blowhole's knees knocked against each other in his trousers and then knocked against Snot's in his and the gerbils slowly, slowly encroached like a furry trickle of evil.

Samantha nudged J.B. who nudged Maciii who didn't need any nudging and was, once more, well ahead of J.B. – he held out the mobile and called J.B.'s phone again.

The shrill ringtone rang out once more. Two hundred gerbil noses twitched, and with a heart-stopping, ear-popping squeaky eek the two hundred ravenous gerbils leapt on Blowhole and Snot! Both baddies were engulfed in an avalanche of nibbles, a whirlpool of pecks and a typhoon of nips. Arms flailed, little legs kicked and bits of baddie body were bitten, battered and bruised.

Maciii high-fived Samantha who turned and high-fived J.B. who turned and high-fived the air next to him and they fled from the restaurant leaving behind a swirling whirl of squealing mayhem.

Chapter Ten
THE CHOCOLATE TAJ MAHAL

The TimTim GPS ZK35/A Multi-Functional Satellite Navigational System sat in the confused hands of Mr Clout who scratched his hand, head and bum as he wrestled with the instructions. The bus he was driving (or would be driving if he hadn't been confused by the satnav) quietly put-putted as the passengers tut-tutted.

"Won't be long now!" he announced to a mirrorful of frustrated faces and jabbed at the tiny screen.

"Please make a U-turn!" ordered the demanding female voice from the box.

"We don't want to miss the countdown launch! Could you please hurry?" hissed a passenger behind his ear.

Mr Clout smiled softly and jabbed some more.

"You have arrived at your destination!" announced the voice.

Mr Clout sighed and sighed again and wondered whether he should have left his job as the school bus driver. Then he remembered he hadn't left the job, he'd been sacked for losing two pupils – two pupils we know very well. He scratched both his ears and went back to his jabbing.

"Toll charge!" snapped the box.

Mr Clout's frustration had been slowly bubbling to the boil for the last few minutes as the gaggle of passengers had tutted, muttered and sighed at his efforts. He just needed one more word from any of them and he'd probably go off pop.

"Hurry!" moaned a dreary voice.

Mr Clout went off pop. He leapt to his feet, turned to the collection of faces and yelled, "Right, that's it! I've had twenty years of jabbering and yabbering voices behind my head. Twenty years of staring at ungrateful faces in the mirror! There's only so much I can take!"

And with that he hurled the satnav through the bus window and thirty pairs of eyes watched its flight and thirty pairs of ears heard it bark,

"You have performed an illegal manoeuvre!"

Mr Clout flopped into his seat and started banging his frustrated forehead against the horn which honked in sympathy.

Honk, honk, honk, honk, honk, honk!

The shuttering doors of the bus suddenly flapped open and a familiar face came face to face with Mr Clout.

"You?" said Mr Clout.

"Great to see you again, Clouty! Did you lose a satnav?" Maciii waved the recently hurled satnav in front of Clouty's eyes. J.B. clambered in behind, scanned the crowd, adjusted his tie and waved. Samantha followed, nudging him out of the way.

"Make it work!" ordered the dreary voice who had just made Mr Clout go pop.

"Sure!" said Maciii. "What's the postcode?"

Mr Clout recited the code he'd already entered a hundred times and the satnav suddenly chirruped, "Turn left at the next junction!"

"I guess you turn left at the next junction!" said Maciii, brightly, handing over the box to Mr Clout, who looked at it like it was a newly hatched chick.

Maciii plunged into the crowd and found himself a seat. J.B. ran a confident hand through his hair and started introducing himself to everyone while Samantha sat wondering how she'd got herself into this mess and how she was going to get herself out before it got messier.

"Nice bus!" nodded J.B. to the owner of the moaning voice who was a youngish man of about twenty and was clearly wondering what a boy half his age was doing sitting next to him.

"What are you doing sitting next to me?" moaned the moaner.

J.B. looked about, leaned closer and said quietly, "Escaping the gerbils!"

The moaner smiled an unsure smile and decided not to talk to J.B. for the rest of the journey. J.B., however, had other plans.

"Yeah, really nice bus. Where's it going?"

"Chocolate Taj Mahal!" the moaner said in a way that implied it was the last thing he would be saying to J.B. for the entire journey. It wasn't.

"Wow!" said J.B. "The Chocolate Taj Mahal. Excellent! The Chocolate Taj Mahal…" There was a long pause during which J.B. repeated the words to himself under his breath. Then something very odd happened. J.B. blinked, blinked again then muttered the words, "Chocolate Taj Mahal!" one more time and then suddenly leapt to his feet and recited to the crowd,

"The Chocolate Taj Mahal – headquarters of Blowhole Enterprises, largest chocolate manufacturer on the planet. Built to house cutting-edge confectionery experiments and develop new strains of global chocolate. Listed on the London Stock Exchange and FTSE 100 Index. Formed from an amalgamation of smaller candy-holding companies and has an annual operating turnover of $673 million. Recently invested 50% of its revenue into developing and promoting…"

And every single voice on the bus finished off his sentence with a joyful shout of, "Downloadable Chocolate!", which they followed with a cheer and smattering of clapping.

Maciii slapped a huge hi-five on J.B. shaking him from his trance, "Great facts, mate!"

Maciii and Samantha exchanged a look, then she said the thought they were both thinking, "So what about the Chocolate Taj Mahal?"

The moaner answered, "That's where we're headed. We are the Official Downloadable Chocolate Fan Club and we're off to witness its official launch!"

A thrilling gasp of delight and adoration ran through the Official Downloadable Chocolate Fan Club as the Chocolate Taj Mahal came into view. Four shimmering brown minarets prodded the bright, white clouds and the bulbous brown dome sat tubbily on top. The headquarters of Blowhole Enterprises was built from heavily reinforced coconcrete - a mixture of chocolate and concrete accidentally developed by the company, who were trying to develop something completely different. This was the epicentre, the hub, the thriving hive of Blowhole Enterprises. This was the place where every order was ordered, every decision decided and every mistake covered-up. The road leading up to the largest chocolate front door you've ever seen (if you ever have seen a chocolate front door) was itself made of coconcrete and was the brownest of browns. Chugging merrily along it was the bus containing the happy throng of visitors chanting, "Downloadable Chocolate!" plus three not so happy visitors wondering whatever was going to happen next.

The chanting crowd were quickly ushered inside by a wodge of stocky, brown-suited security guards, wearing brown sunglasses and chattering into brown headpieces. Everything about the building was plush, expensive and very, very brown. The crowd stood and gazed and oohed and aahed at the immense chocolatiness of it all. J.B.

smiled, Samantha grimaced and Maciii made a note of all the escape routes.

Suddenly, a tap-tapping noise was heard followed by a squealing of electronics followed by a meek voice saying, "Testing…one…two…three…is this on?" Samantha looked about her sensing she recognised the voice. So did Maciii. It was unmistakable.

"Who's that voice?" asked J.B.

"Good afternoon, everyone, and welcome to the Chocolate Taj Mahal, and the birthplace of Downloadable Chocolate!"

The throng clapped and cheered and even whooped a little.

"My name is Dwayne Deek, Head of E-Tweaking and Choc-Enhancements. As our CEO, Oleg Blowhole, appears to be mysteriously detained it falls to me to welcome you all. Welcome!"

The nervous face of Deek, the bespectacled geek from St Smugg's, looked down on them from a huge brown HD screen on a far wall. Another face came onto the screen and hastily whispered in Deek's ear.

"Oh, yes, yes, I nearly forgot. It's three hours to the launch of Downloadable Chocolate across the globe. So let's start the countdown clock!" Deek gestured and shimmered away to be replaced by a digital clock with the digits

3.00

which a second later were replace by the digits

2.59

and then almost the same amount of time later replaced by

2.58

which was followed by

2.57

You get the idea.

In a hushed group Maciii, J.B. and Samantha watched all the goings-on going-on. They watched the Fan Club being issued with sweets and souvenirs to celebrate their visit and saw them merrily trading and chatting and having a jolly time. Maciii couldn't help noticing the guards spread out all around – each cautiously scanning the scene from behind their brown glasses. Occasionally, one mumbled into his headpiece, did a little bit of pointing and the order reshuffled. The group of Chocolate fans were being watched very, very carefully, but Maciii couldn't work out why.

He beckoned the other two closer and whispered,

"I've got a plan!"

"Excellent!" smiled J.B.

"What is it?" whispered Samantha.

"You stay here and mingle with these people. Try and find out what you can and why they're being watched so carefully. J.B. and I'll go and poke about and see if we can find it."

"It?" smiled J.B.

"The Choc Chip!" hissed Maciii, then checked no one had heard him.

"Oh, the…!" J.B. didn't complete his sentence as Samantha clasped a silencing hand over his mouth.

"Stay in touch!" said Samantha, waggling her phone at them, and, releasing J.B., she plunged into the crowd and quickly began introducing herself to all the Chocolate fans yacking endless questions. Once she had engaged them all in delightful chatter she allowed herself a crafty glance to see if the boys had gone. They had!

'Private – Keep Out – No entry to non-Blowhole Employees – Trespassers will be arrested, sued, jailed and sternly shouted at.'

J.B. read the sign and sighed, "How disappointing! Guess we can't go in. However are we to find the Chip now?"

"Like this"

Maciii was standing before him dressed in the bright brown uniform of a Blowhole employee – exactly the same as the ones they'd seen outside.

"Wow!" said J.B. "Nice fit! Where'd you get it?"

Maciii pointed at the lock of the door he had just picked which now hung wide open.

"Wow! Do you think they have anything from Harrods?"

Maciii bundled his buddy into the uniform room and within minutes J.B. was admiring himself in the mirror. He was clad from head to foot in brown.

"Hate brown!" he said, flicking up his collar. "What I really need is a fine silk…!"

"This is not a fashion parade! We have to find the…"

"Grimly and Fiddle?"

The voice came from a smallish man with a surprisingly flat head and a nose which looked like it would fit snugly into a sock. He eyed them up and down, then referred to the clipboard he'd be been holding to his chest like a shield.

"Grimly and Fiddle?" he asked again, his voice like an

exhausted moose.

"Yes!" said Maciii.

"No!" said J.B. at exactly the same time. An awkward moment hung in the air as the boys wondered what to say next.

"No!" said Maciii.

"Yes!" said J.B. at exactly the same time.

The flat-headed man tapped his pen on the clipboard.

"Which is it?"

J.B. was humming quietly to himself hoping the man would go away, but Maciii said, "I'm Grimly and he's Fiddle!"

"Cornelius Fiddle!" J.B. heard himself saying and wished he hadn't.

The flat-headed man leaned towards them and said in a conspiratorial voice, "It keeps going ping!"

"Oh dear," said J.B.

"I've cross-loaded the OS Motherboard, inputted 10k RAM and stripped the lithium ionizers…"

He was speaking a language J.B. couldn't understand but Maciii could.

"So what does it do now?" asked Maciii.

The flat-headed man looked about again and said, "It goes ping! Today of all days. Good job you're here. Can you fix it?"

"Sure!" said Maciii, confidently.

"Sure!" said J.B, less confidently, then added, "Is it a big ping or a little ping or perhaps a kind of medium ping?"

The flat-headed man strode off, beckoning with his clipboard for them to follow. They followed.

105

The flat-headed man strode down squeaky clean corridor after squeaky clean corridor, past nameless doors and blurred windows.

J.B. was trying to shrug a questioning shrug at Maciii as they strode behind, but it wasn't easy to do, so he resorted to hissing under his breath.

"What is going on?"

Maciii hissed back, "He thinks we're two computer engineers because of the uniforms! Just stick with me!"

The flat-headed man halted outside one of the hundred white and nameless doors and referred to his clipboard.

"Secret numeric code – same one for all the doors here!" he winked at them. "Can't reveal it to anyone otherwise I lose my job. Does that look like a 3 or 6 to you?"

Maciii looked at the clipboard.

"7!" he answered.

The flat-headed man stabbed the numbers into a numeric keylock outside the door and waited. And waited.

Then finally said, "A sort of medium ping, I guess!"

J.B. was writing the words 'medium ping' on his sleeve as the bright, white door slid hissingly open.

The room into which they stepped fizzed and buzzed with pings of all shapes, sizes and volumes. A couple of bleeps and the occasional peep. The entire room was a cavern of flashing, dashing blue screens. Peering into each was a boggle-eyed operative tip-tapping away at their keyboards like vultures trying to crack eggs.

"Blowhole Enterprises Network Hub!" announced the flat-headed man gesturing with his clipboard and narrowly missing another worker. "The communication epicentre of the entire Blowhole operation. Goldenbum controls us; we control everything else. And this is my work station!"

J.B. moved to the laptop and listened to the ping and said officially, "Oh, that's certainly medium!"

"Can you fix it?" asked flat head.

"Can we fix it?" asked J.B.

"Sure we can!" finished Maciii. "Just give us some time!"

The flat-headed man nodded, bowed slightly and disappeared into the throng of buzzing and fizzing and tapping.

"I thought we were going to find the Choc Chip!" J.B. whispered.

"We're about to!" Maciii whispered back.

And with those words Maciii clicked his knuckles, his tongue and his mouse and plunged his fingers into a tip-tapping Riverdance across the keyboard. He circled his mouse faster and faster. He leapt through security firewalls and sidestepped ID protection like he'd been doing it all his life; and he had. He debugged, reprogrammed, interfaced, flashed and Javaed. His eyes were glued to the flickering screen as windows snapped open and closed and a tumbling avalanche of statics, graphs and databases unfurled before him.

J.B. watched in awe as the dazzling display of IT skills reached its climax. Maciii jabbed, grabbed and stabbed at more keys, cracked his mouse like a whip and then suddenly stopped still and waited. The laptop hummed and purred and then gave off one huge, shrill, "Ping!"

"It pinged!" whooped J.B. "Was that a good ping or a bad ping?"

Maciii nodded towards a trilling printer spilling out sheets of paper.

"Good!"

Maciii leaned over and snatched at the papers, inspecting them closely. "Perfect!"

"Perfect!" J.B. whooped again. "What's perfect?"

Maciii held the papers up to J.B.'s inquisitive eyes. Like most things in his life they made little sense, but he wasn't going to let that spoil his fun.

"Perfect! What is it?"

Maciii lowered his voice and the papers.

"Map to the location of the Choc Chip!"

"It's still pinging!" said the moose-like voice of the flat-headed man, who had just appeared at their side. "Stop it pinging!"

Maciii grabbed J.B.'s arm, muttered, "Lunchtime!" and dragged himself and his companion from the bleeping, peeping, pinging computer room. Now to find the Choc Chip!

Chapter Eleven
DOWNLOADABLE CHOCOLATE
UNWRAPPED

Dwayne Deek sat in a quiet corner of the Taj Mahal foyer as members of the Official Downloadable ChocolateTM Fan Club danced, bopped and gyrated to the sounds of the loudest music his ears had ever endured. A sumptuous chocolate buffet was laid out before their gleeful, popping eyes – each and every finger dipping, scooping and poking the latest chocolate creations from Blowhole Enterprises. Deek hated parties, meetings, get-togethers; in fact, any sort of social event requiring eye contact and interaction - he was more interested in chatting on the Geek2Geek app on his new e-phone. He pecked and poked at the screen hoping to find some interesting conversation about molecular nutritional restructuring or the latest gossip on E-numbers. Instead he heard a word in his ear.

"Deeky!"

Deek leapt to his feet, accidentally plopping his e-phone in a nearby trifle, and spun round to see who was shrieking his name.

"Darling!"

The shriek came from the chocolatey mouth of Samantha Clunk, "We went to St Smugg's together, remember?"

Deek scooped the dripping e-phone from the trifle and said, "It was only 3.4 weeks ago. Of course, I remember!" He wondered whether to lick the phone clean but decided it was better manners to wipe it on his tie. So he did.

"And what are you doing here, Miss Clunk?"

Samantha nibbled at a chocolate button. "Oh the usual - mixing, milling, chocolate hobnobbing. How about you?"

"I work here!"

"OMG-ultra! How cool is that? This place is fascinating!"

"I know. I work here! I know the place inside out!"

"Way cool!" she cooed, wiping a little something from Deek's cheek. No one had ever wiped a little anything from his cheek before and he was not sure what to do.

"Why did you just do that?" he asked, flatly.

"You had a bit of trifle there."

"Were you being kind?"

"Yes."

"Then I think my response has to be thank you."

He gazed at her as if he was examining a new strain of hydrogenated fat and wondered what it would do next.

"Must be fascinating work!" was what it did next.

"Yes, it is fascinating work. All the really important work happens in the back rooms."

"Really?" Samantha drew herself a little closer. "I would love…L.U.V…to see the back rooms!"

Deek nodded to himself and continued to examine her as if through a microscope. Samantha leaned further forward and wiped his cheek a second time. Then she smiled. In the awkward moment that followed, Deek's eyebrows raised and lowered, his eyes gazed into nothingness, and his fingers fingered his endless pen collection. He was thinking. Then he said,

"Would you like to see the back rooms?"

The bleeping, peeping, blipping Computer Room, which J.B. and Maciii had just left, was still bleeping, peeping and blipping as Deek and Samantha arrived. The same googled-eyed faces were staring at the same blue screens and the same poky fingers pecked at the same keyboards.

"Wow-big time!" squealed Samantha, whirling round to take it all in. "I love…L…U…V…computers. They're so…cute!"

She was stopped mid-whirl by a man with a surprisingly flat head.

"You haven't seen Grimly and Fiddle, have you?" he asked, moosey.

Deek shook his head.

"It's still going ping!" he muttered, and scuttled away.

"So what exactly is this place?" Samantha grabbed Deek's hand.

"Well…", and "Well" was the last word Samantha understood as Deek plunged into a techno-babble lecture. Jargon and buzzwords spun around her head as Deek rattled on and on. Words like 'Polarity Reversal Systems', 'Entropic Vector Stabilisers', 'Dummy Emulsifier Inversion' and 'Sugar Coating Cortex' all bubbled from his mouth.

Samantha nodded as wisely as she could with each new phrase. She hmmmed knowingly when Deek said, 'Functional Gravitic Index Amalgamator Loop!' then waited for his next words.

"It's as simple as that really!"

"Wow – you make it so easy to understand! All to make Downloadable Chocolate. Love it!"

Then Deek did something he hadn't done for a very long time. He giggled. He covered his mouth, but then giggled again. Then he smirked.

"Look at you!" shrieked Samantha. "Loving the smirk. What's so funny?"

Deek looked from side to side to make sure no one could hear what he was about to say next, because what he was about to say he'd never said before in his life. Out loud. Ever.

"There's no such thing…" He giggled again, "There's no such thing," He giggled some more, "…as Downloadable Chocolate!" And then he giggled lots more.

Samantha Clunk, secret agent, immediately started to calculate what she'd been told while Samantha Clunk, party guest, simply shrieked, "OMG-max! That's so cool. LOL!!"

Deek nodded, hardly controlling his gurgling giggles.

"Only me and Oleg Blowhole know it. Everyone thinks once they log on to the website they get Downloadable Chocolate straight to their PCs."

"And they won't??"

Deek shook his head.

"And you keep all their money?"

Deek nodded his head.

"This is…like…the best thing ever!"

Samantha Clunk, secret agent, was thinking what to do with this vital piece of information whilst Samantha Clunk, party guest, suddenly shouted, "OMG100 I love this song! Come and dance!" She knew very well what Deek would say to the invitation.

"No thank you," he said. She was right. And Samantha danced from the Computer Room, danced through the thronging crowd of party goings, danced out of the door and stopped dancing when she arrived on the empty fire exit.

She snatched her mobile phone from her pocket and ran her finger down her contacts until she found J.B.'s listing. She pressed it.

"Pick up! Pick up!" she whispered, urgently. The phone stopped ringing. "J.B.? It's Samantha Clunk – don't say anything just listen…"

Chapter Twelve
BLING BLING!

Oleg Blowhole sat in a seething cloud of muttering venom in the back of his speeding Rolls Royce beneath 37 sticking plasters covering his face, knees, toes and other parts of his nibbled body.

"Ow!" he squealed as Snot ran the sleek, brown and very expensive car over yet another painful speed bump. He would have apologised but Blowhole had earlier slapped a silencing plaster over his servant's mouth. The two plasters over Blowhole's eyebrows wiggled and waggled up and down as he schemed vengeful revenge on Maciii, J.B. and Samantha. The car skidded to a screeching halt outside the Chocolate Taj Mahal and brown-clad guards scrambled over themselves to open the door to their boss. Each saluted as Oleg Blowhole emerged like something exhumed from a Pharaoh's tomb.

"Unload Goldenbum! Get it inside!" ordered Blowhole, blowing a flapping plaster from his top lip. Within seconds scurrying guards, accompanied by a scuttling Snot, were sweatingly dragging Goldenbum from the car toward the Chocolate Taj Mahal. Blowhole strode on ahead and gleefully surveyed the swinging Launch Party.

On the podium a bling-riddled DJ was gyrating to cheesy pop music and inciting the Fan Club to whoop if they loved chocolate. The clapping chocoholics whooped louder and louder as disco sounds exploded from the speakers. The DJ was about to lead the writhing crowd in a chocolate hokey-kokey when the finger of Blowhole stabbed the stop button. The silence that filled the foyer, for a moment seemed louder than the music that preceded it. A few confused grunts broke the silence and in the distance was the faint sound of a computer going ping. Blowhole snatched the microphone from the confused hands of the DJ and spoke.

"Friends, chocolate lovers, candy fans, lovers of all things brown and sticky. Today is the day. Within a few moments the ticking of the countdown clock will be completed and each and every one of you will witness the Global Launch of Downloadable Chocolate! The Greatest Confectionery on the Planet!" He thrust his hands triumphantly in the air expecting an ovation of approving applause. He didn't get any. He repeated the last six words of the sentence again and did some more hand thrusting but the silence remained silent until a small voice at the back shouted, "Sorry. Who are you?" and in the distance echoed another ping.

"It's me!" yelped Blowhole, pointing at himself to make his point. "Me!"

The gaggle of chocolate lovers shrugged confusingly and a few puzzled bottom lips jutted out.

"Who?" asked a voice from the back.

"ME!!" repeated Blowhole, pointing with both fingers now.

"You're covered in sticking plasters!" shouted the voice.

"Wait a minute!" yelled Blowhole and slowly and painfully began peeling the plasters from his eyebrows removing a hefty chunk of hair as he did.

"Don't you recognise me?" He wiggled his eyebrows irresistibly.

"Oleg Blowhole!!" the chocoholics chorused as he wiggled and they clapped and whooped and whistled their hero.

"Thank you! Thank you! Now where was I?" He was about to relaunch his stirring speech when there was a bleeping. For a moment his heart stopped but his head raced ahead. The last time he'd heard that ringtone he'd been accosted by two hundred of the most vicious sets of teeth ever to nibble a toe. He shuddered and reached for the phone, peeled a sticking plaster from his eye and peered at the caller ID.

SAMANTHA CLUNK

"Well, well, well!" he muttered then said to the crowd, "Shhh!" They shushed as he placed the phone to his ear and soon realised he couldn't hear a thing because of the plasters. He flicked to hands-free instead.

And the words that followed echoed down the microphone through the loudspeakers and into the intrigued ears of every member of the Downloadable Chocolate Fan Club.

"J.B.? It's Samantha Clunk – don't say anything just listen. I've just been talking to Dwayne Deek, Head of E-Tweaking and Choc-Enhancements at Blowhole Enterprises? You are not going to believe this! There is no such thing as Downloadable Chocolate! It's a scam! Blowhole has convinced everyone it really exists, but it doesn't! All he's doing is making people pay online for a product that is not going to be delivered! There's no such thing as Downloadable Chocolate! J.B.? J.B.? Are you getting all this?"

Oleg Blowhole slowly lifted his plastered eyes from the phone and found his angry gaze met by the angrier gaze of the Downloadable Chocolate Fan Club – each and every pair of eyes belonging to a frustrated fan waiting for an explanation. He rummaged through his brain to find the right words.

"Ahh…" was the first word he found, followed by, "Errrmm!" and ending with, "Er…!"

"Now I know what you're all thinking…" he stumbled. "But let me explain. How can I explain?" His eyes fell on a fire alarm button on the desk. "Perhaps this will help!" and he swatted it like a fly

WHOOP!! WHOOP!! WHOOP!! WHOOP!!

CLEAR THE AREA!! CLEAR THE AREA!! CLEAR THE AREA!!

The piercing command shattered the awkward silence and, like a well-drilled regiment of chocolate soldiers, the brown-clad guards snapped into action. They began tugging and grabbing and shifting and pushing and poking and prodding.

WHOOP!! WHOOP!! WHOOP!! WHOOP!!

Snot appeared by his master's side amidst the chaos, unaware of the happenings that had just happened and said, "I've plugged in your bum!" and Blowhole tweaked his inverted nose.

"Eeek!"

"We've been tumbled, doofus!" he hissed. "Downloadable Chocolate has leaked!!"

Snot was still confused.

"Shall I get some paper towels?"

WHOOP!! WHOOP!! WHOOP!!

The guards were pushing and shoving the fans but were unsure where to push and shove them to, so while they waited to be told they pushed and shoved some more.

"Maciii, JB and Samantha Clunk are in the building! Find them and bring them to me!"

WHOOP!! WHOOP!! WHOOP!!

"What shall we do with this lot?"

Despite the whooping and shouting all about him Blowhole drummed his fingers quietly on his chin and thought, then he finally said, softly, "Lock them in the Solidifier."

"Pardon?"

"Lock them in the Solidifier!!"

WHOOP!! WHOOP!! WHOOP!!

"Not the Solidifier?"

"Yes, the Solidi…I'm not going to repeat it a third time! Go!"

And Snot went.

The Diffraction X-90B/S Optical Fibre Core Repository sat humming in the centre of the dark room of which Maciii had just cracked the lock. In the centre hung the Choc Chip, suspended in an intricate, interwoven lattice of green laser beams like a confused shrimp caught in a glowing fishing net.

"Wow!" hushed J.B. "It's like a giant safe made from lasers. What is it?"

"Well, it's a giant safe made from lasers. You're getting good!" Maciii slid over to the complex control panel and started calculating his next move.

"Can't we just grab it?"

"If you did you'd never pick your nose again!"

J.B.'s quizzical look grew more quizzical as Maciii drew a pen from his friend's pocket.

"Watch!"

He tossed the pen through the air. It hit a beam, popped, fizzed and shredded into a thousand particles which floated gently to the floor.

"Ouch!" squeaked J.B. then touched his nose with his finger, "Double ouch!"

"All we have to do is get the Choc Chip out of there and back to MI3(and a bit)."

Far in the distance at the other end of the Chocolate Taj Mahal a whoop-whooping could be faintly heard.

"Sounds like the party's really starting! What you going to do?"

Maciii scanned the control panel. "I'm going to sub-serve the photon emissions by switching the optical output coupler with plasma resonator thus dio-directing the exponential frequencies and freeing the Chip for a nanosecond!"

"Wow!" said J.B. "A whole nanosecond! That's not long, right? What do I do?"

"Catch it when the lights go out!"

J.B. hurried over to the glowing repository and cupped his hands underneath the Choc Chip and between the piercing green beams.

"The Chip will still be in a Quantum state when it's released. Catch it at the right time and you'll be fine!"

"And if I catch it at the wrong time?"

"You'll never pick your nose again!"

J.B. felt a bead of sweat trickle down his forehead. He took a deep breath.

"Ready!" he said, finally.

Maciii ran his hands along the ergonomic keyboard, stabbed a few keys, waited and stabbed them again.

"Come on, come on!"

There was a reluctant click and a thudding judder. J.B. started.

"It's going to be fine!" Maciii jabbed another key. "Okay, I'm sub-serving…" He took a deep breath, "…now!"

Suddenly every beam on the repository snapped off plunging the room into darkness and then just as quickly snapped back on, blazing the room with green light once more.

"J.B.? J.B.? You okay!"

There was a silence then a small giggle and J.B. said, "Guess I can still pick my nose!" He showed Maciii the Choc Chip safely in his hands. "Let's get outta here!"

Chapter Thirteen
DUNKED IN HOT CHOCOLATE

The Solidifier 5000X was a huge, hollow reinforced glass tank built to withstand pressures of 1.25 metric tons per cm2. It was originally designed to solidify 75,000 litres of liquid chocolate within 2.3 seconds – the fastest and most efficient system on the planet. Blowhole was pleased with his Solidifier and even more pleased the Downloadable Chocolate Fan Club had been imprisoned in it.

"Ouch!" yelped the sweating brown-clad guard as he prodded the final finger of the final hand of the final member of the Fan Club into the Solidifier then clanged the door shut, slammed the bolt across, sighed like a deflating tyre and mopped his brow and armpits. All the guards carried out their boss's orders through a combination of persuasion ("It's for your own safety!"), shouting ("Do you want me to get angry??") and prodding with a stick ("I'm prodding you for your own good!"). Eventually the coaxed, confused, cajoled Fan Club had been herded up and slammed safely away.

Meanwhile, not far away, the CEO of Blowhole Enterprises was wrestling with his servant.

"Hold it still, Snot! Hold it still!" squawked Blowhole to his fretting, sweating servant, who was jiggling an e-phone before his boss's annoyed eyes. "What is it? What is it?"

"I got footage! Look!" Blowhole stilled Snot's wavering hand with a stealthy arm-lock and gazed into the e-phone which was in the middle of unfurling footage taken from a CCTV camera in the Computer Room. The raw and static picture zoomed in on Samantha Clunk and Dwayne Deek discussing the scam of Downloadable Chocolate. Blowhole hissed, swore, hissed again, threw the e-phone on the floor with a clatter then slapped Snot.

"What did I do?" whinged his servant, rubbing his head.

"Nothing! And don't do it again!"

Blowhole strode back and forth before the towering Solidifier oblivious to shouts, complaints and muffled moans from within. He spun on the spot and strode back and forth again. Inside his plastered head his pensive mind was rapidly weighing up all the ups and downs. What had gone wrong? This was his master plan! How could he fail? How could he EVER fail? He nibbled his bottom lip, then his fingernail then he plucked at his eyebrow and nibbled a hair. It helped him think.

He suddenly turned on the spot and addressed the inmates of the Solidifier.

"You cretinous bunch of snivelling doofuses! Now I can tell you everything. There is no such thing as Downloadable Chocolate! It's a scam, a wheeze, a figment of my staggeringly impressive imagination! I have convinced the entire planet of its existence!"

He cackled manically then cackled again because he liked it.

"By the time that clock…" He pointed in the wrong direction, looked about and repointed, "…that clock reaches zero, millions of dollars, francs, euros, yen, rupees, rubles and twongs will come sloshing into my Swiss Bank Account and there's nothing you can do about it! Nothing!"

Blowhole's slithering eyes scanned the confused, bemused and disappointed faces behind the glass.

"Within minutes I shall be gone! Never to be seen again!" He lowered his voice and whispered to Snot, "Go get the Choc Pod!"

"Not the Choc Pod?"

Blowhole poked two fingers down Snot's nostrils and snarled,

"I'm not repeating it!"

"Dorry!" said Snot, carefully removing his boss's fingers and scurrying away.

"Guards!"

The brown-clad guards fell into what they thought was a well-organised line up and saluted.

"Flood the Solidifier!" ordered Blowhole. "Flood it with the stickiest, gooiest liquid chocolate we have!"

The eyes of the guards leapt from side to side trying to see if the other guards had heard what they had just heard, and they had.

"Just up to their necks!" Blowhole relented. "Then solidify the chocolate!" And with those orders hanging in the air he strode off after Snot.

Maciii skidded to a halt outside the giant Solidifier as Blowhole was issuing his final order and flouncing off. J.B. skidded into him.

"Mind the Choc Chip!" hissed his buddy.

J.B. padded his breast pocket.

"Safe!" he announced.

As he threw open the far fire exit door, Blowhole turned to survey his crumbling empire one final time. His jelly bean eyes swept the room, almost catching sight of the boys, who swiftly dodged back into the corridor.

"Mind the Choc Chip!" hissed J.B.

Maciii took the Chip from his friend's pocket and placed it in his own.

"Safe!"

The clanging door announced Blowhole's departure and Maciii and J.B. peeked out then crept out into the corridor.

SLOP, SLOP, SLOP!

The sound of gallons and gallons and gallons of dribbling chocolate goo chugging and glugging into the Solidifier met their ears and the sight of sticky, brown slush engulfing the frightened feet of the Fan Club met their eyes.

SLOP, SLOP, SLOP!

"We're getting candied!" one frightened voice screamed, banging her fist on the glass.

"We're going to be fermented!" screamed another as the chocolate liquid started to move up their legs.

Maciii looked at J.B. who looked at Maciii who looked at Samantha, who'd just scrabbled into the room, who looked at Dwayne Deek, who'd just scrabbled in behind her.

"We've got to do something!" shouted Samantha.

"Yes, something!" agreed J.B. "What something?"

Maciii took over. "Dwayne, J.B. - divert the guards! Sam and I'll unlock the door! Go!"

And with that the group scattered in opposite directions like startled ants.

By now the guards, who had been very loyal to Blowhole Enterprises, were slowly beginning to realise they might be losing out.

"Do we still get paid?" asked one.

"Probably not," said another. "I'm going to nab as much choc as I can then leg it!"

Suddenly a voice rang out over the loudspeakers.

"Whose boss ran off then?" J.B.'s voice taunted down the microphone, which Dwayne had just plugged in. "Who's not getting any money? Who's left with choc-choc on their little faces?" Then he started making that noise people make when they really want to annoy people and it really annoyed the guards. They lurched towards the DJ podium and started heckling and abusing J.B. and grabbing at his cable. J.B. taunted and hopped about out of their reach and taunted them some more, at the same time keeping a

125

sly eye on Samantha and Maciii.

At the Solidifier door Maciii was staring at the numeric lock keypad as the desperate faces of the Fan Club pleaded for release. The chocolate sauce glugged further and further up their bodies.

SLOP, SLOP, SLOP.

"Hurry!" shouted Samantha.

Maciii took a deep breath, blocked out the chaos around him and focused. Focused like he'd never focused before in his life.

"Think, Maciii!" he said, under his breath. Suddenly his mind flashed back to something the flat-headed man had said before they went into the computer room. The security number on his clipboard was the same for every door in the place. But what was the number, Maciii? Think! He fixed his mind on the clipboard and visualised it, conjuring it up in his mind. Then he stabbed some numbers into the numeric door lock.

Whrrr! Click!

The door sprung open releasing a tidal wave of sloshy chocolate sauce followed by some very grateful Fan Club members. Screams of delight and cries of "Freedom!" resounded as member after member waded out of the Solidifier pumping Maciii's hand as they went.

"Thank you! Thank you! Thank you!"

Maciii nodded gleefully as they slopped and sloshed away and turned to Samantha and said, "Guess what we found?"

"What?"

"The Choc Chip!" And he reached into his pocket. "Wait, it's gone! It had everything on it. It must have jumped out when they shook my hand! Help me search!"

He sploshed to his knees in the gooey sauce, scooping up pints of sauce and straining it through his frantic fingers.

"It doesn't matter!" yelled Samantha, closing the Solidifier door and stemming any further chocolate flow.

"Of course it matters – get on your knees and help!"

"No, really, Maciii. Deek told me!"

"We've got to get it back!"

"There's no such thing as Downloadable Chocolate. Anything on the Chip would be useless. It was a scam!"

"A what?"

"Blowhole was fooling everyone. He made us all think the Chip was important, but it wasn't!"

Maciii was scooping and straining and glooping handful after handful, but as Samantha's words fell on his ears the scooping and the straining and the glooping got slower and slower.

"You mean…we stole the Chip…for nothing?"

"Well, yes! But the system is still in place! By the time the countdown clock reaches zero – the money from everyone who ever logged onto the Downloadable Chocolate website will be transferred to Blowhole's secret bank account! And what controls the website?"

Maciii jumped to his feet with gooey brown sauce plopping off his hands and knees and said softly,

"Goldenbum!!"

"Please climb aboard!"

The voice came from Dwayne Deek who, with J.B. at his side, had just skidded to a choccy stop in his brown Golf Buggy.

"I told J.B. everything about the Choc Chip!" he said.

"Seems that little jape was a complete waste of time! All we have to do now it disarm…"

The other three jumped aboard and shouted,

"Goldenbum!"

Deek hit the accelerator, skidded the wheel and sprayed sloppy gobs of chocolate goo in the faces of the encroaching guards who threw their arms up in submission as the buggy sped out of sight. The Chocolate Buggy swerved round corner after corner as they wildly whizzed towards the Goldenbum Room with the sound of the countdown clock ringing in their ears and getting closer and closer to zero with each count.

Suddenly, coming towards them in the same corridor was another vehicle. It looked like a cross between a high-speed racing car and an Easter Egg.

"The Choc Pod!" Deek announced. "I hope there's enough room!" And he floored the escalator pedal lurching the buggy forward.

In the Choc Pod, Blowhole was berating Snot and urging him to go faster, but Snot was too busy pointing out what was headed towards them and wondering what everyone else was wondering too.

Was there enough room?

Closer and closer they came.

Each occupant of each vehicle braced themselves as they passed within millimetres of each other. And in the fragment of a second in which two pairs of villainous eyes met the gaze of four pairs of heroic eyes all six villainous and heroic mouths shouted, "It's them!"

Chapter Fourteen
SPLOSH!!

Goldenbum sat defiant and god-like at the heart of the chocolate catacomb. A congregation of cables and wires snaked about its feet plugged into thousands of humming sockets. Bleeping, blinking routers and modems trilled and peeped before it like slaves praising their master.

By the entrance J.B. and Samantha kept watch as the fingers of Maciii and Dwayne Deek hung over the keyboard control panel like little stalactites and the glowing golden light from its screens lit up their anxious faces.

"Okay, we need to reroute all the data packeting protocols!" the hushed voice of Deek echoed around the cavernous room.

"Shouldn't we sub-net the firewalls first?" asked Maciii intently.

"No time, there's nearly a million users online now! I'll start rerouting, you integrate the open source destination codes!"

"We're debiting all monies back to the original buyers, yeah?"

"How cool is that?"

The fingers of Maciii and Deek tore across the control panels cancelling and readdressing every single payment addressed to Blowhole Enterprises.

"Just rerouted 275,000 transfers from Paymate!" whooped Maciii.

"30,000 hacked back to Floyds Bank!" Deek whooped back.

The countdown clock continued its slide down as Maciii shouted,

"59,000 charge backed to all Fastercard accounts!"

"Pretty impressive!" said J.B., running his hand through his hair and smiling at Samantha.

"I have never seen anyone work a keyboard like that pair!" she replied.

"Oh, them?" J.B. briefly glanced at Maciii and J.B. "No, I meant the way you keep watch. Holding that door and so forth. Very impressive." He nodded at the moon shining in through a far window. "After all this madness is over would you like to go for a walk with me?"

Samantha smiled, playfully tapped J.B. on the chin and said, "Don't be stupid!"

"115,000 returned to all purchases made on Freebay!"

"You cretinous bunch of snivelling doofuses!" the thundering voice of Oleg Blowhole filled the room and every slithering syllable twanged off the walls. J.B. and Samantha looked around confused, Maciii's fingers dangled in silence and a trickle of cold sweat ran down Deek's leg. Had they been caught?

"Now I have you incarcerated I can tell you everything!" continued the unmistakable snarl. "And everything you've heard is true! True! There IS no such thing as Downloadable Chocolate!"

"Of course!" Samantha plunged her hand in her pocket and pulled out her e-phone, which was bleating out Blowhole's rant. "I taped him shouting at the people in the Solidifier. Thought it'd make great evidence!" She stabbed the pause button silencing Blowhole.

A huge sigh swept through the room and Maciii and Deek's fingers pounced back on their task keeping neck and neck with the countdown clock. Rubles, dollars, francs, yen and euros all bounced safely back to their owners.

5

"Nearly there!"

4

"Just one payee to return!"

3

"What's the address?"

2

"snot@stsmuggs.com!"

1

"Leave it!"

0

Maciii and Deek flopped back into the huge arms of Goldenbum and gleefully hi-fived each other.

"Job done!" yelped Maciii.

"Almost!" said Samantha, nestling between them hi-fiving. J.B. sat awkwardly on the arm panel, bleeping a few buttons.

"What you mean 'almost'? We just saved thousands of people from losing their money and redirected it all back to their accounts!"

"But Blowhole is still on the run!"

"Oh!"

"No probs!" announced Deek, jumping up and over to a nearby cabinet. "GHz3 Wireless HD 3D Co-Polarisation E-goggles. Blowhole uses them when he wants to take over someone's work station but can't be bothered getting up!"

"So?"

"I think I might have another use for them!"

"Go faster, go faster, go faster!" snapped Blowhole, swaying back and forth in his seat and chewing his seatbelt.

"I can't get the pedal down any further, boss!"

The Choc Pod was a hi-tech trove of state-of-the-art speedery. Snot's eyes stared out through a blistered hood on which an array of figures and graphs popped up and down charting their speeding escape. Beyond the figures, through the reddened glass, he could see the chocolate driveway trailing on up ahead and the exit gate a little further. Either side of it disgruntled security guards were sloping home with arms full of chocolate goodies making rude gestures as their ex-boss flew by.

"Faster, doofus, faster! Or I'll tweak your nose!"

"It doesn't go any faster!!!" yelled Snot, when suddenly all the figures on the screen started flickering and tumbling over. Graphs started inverting and little lights that hadn't blinked before started blinking. And more importantly the entire escape pod was starting to slow down.

J.B. looked like a bug; a huge boggled-eyed bug with its tongue sticking out in concentration. The massive e-goggles strapped to his head gave him a direct virtual view from the dashboard of the Choc Pod and the wireless joystick gave him complete control of the Choc Pod's directional unit. Pity he'd never driven before.

"Ha!" he yelled, as he jiggled and wiggled the stick back and forth. "Just worked out what that bit does. Okay, what's this do?"

"Snot? Why are we slowing down and why is this seat massaging my bottom?"

Snot shrugged, jabbed at some buttons and slowly told himself something he'd never, ever dare tell his boss. He'd lost control of the Choc Pod!

"Okay, okay! So I'm slowly turning the entire Pod now!" J.B. peered intently into the goggles as he rotated the joystick 360O. "Now all I have to do is accelerate...oops! That's the e-pod. Think I've just given them some music. Okay, here's the accelerator...."

"Is this Brahms, Snot? Aarrggghhhh!"

133

Snot's and Blowhole's bodies were suddenly slapped with a 5.4 g-force impact as J.B. wrenched their speed up to 160kph in under 0.6 second.

"Arrrrrrgggggggggggggggggggggggggggggggh!!" screamed Blowhole.

"Moooooooozzzzzzzzzzaaaaarrrrrtttttt!!" screamed Snot.

The Choc Pod shot like a terrified coconut fired from a really angry catapult and sped back up the driveway, smashed through the Chocolate Doors and juddered to a halt above the Solidifier.

"What do I do now?" demanded J.B. as he viewed the tottering Pod on the brink of sploshing nose-first into the bubbling chocolate sauce below. Maciii, Samantha and Deek, who'd been watching everything on a flat-screen monitor, all replied in unison.

"Dunk them!"

"Sure?"

"But wait till we get there!" and they ran out the door.

"Do something, Snot!" hissed Blowhole, clutching the seat.

"I am doing something and I'm doing it in my trousers!"

Deek cranked the handbrake of the Chocolate Buggy as it skidded to a halt before the Solidifier. Out hopped Samantha and Maciii slightly slipping in the runny residue of chocolate sauce.

"OMG!" shouted Samantha.

"OMG1000!" yelled Deek.

The Choc Pod wobbled and tottered precipitously on the very edge of the Solidifier. One slip, one false move, one slight tremor would send the pod sploshing into the Choc Sauce. The pod creaked and squeaked as metal grated against metal. Inside were two frozen faces, hugging the door handles not daring to move, speak or even breathe.

J.B. licked his lips, firmly grasped the joystick and with one firm movement thrust it forward.

"Aaaaaarrrrrrggghhhhhhh!!"
"Aaaaaaaaaaaarrrrrrrrrrrggggggggggggggggghhhh!"
And with one almighty globby splosh the Choc Pod ker-plopped nose-first in the ocean of bubbling chocolate sauce, bobbed about slightly then slowly plop-plop-plopped below the brown waves.

Maciii, Deek and Samantha whooped, squawked and bellowed with delight and hi-tenned like manic cheerleaders. Within seconds J.B. was by their side watching the Choc Pod slowly sinking like a chocolate-coated Titanic.

"What now?" asked Samantha.

"We check they're okay!" said Maciii, moving closer and peering through the glass.

Suddenly, two brown and sticky heads emerged and two pairs of white eyes popped open looking like icing on a cupcake.

"They're getting out!"

"So then we do this!"

Maciii slapped the solidify button. 2000 megawatts of

quantum electricity suddenly fizzed through the Solidifier cooling the chocolate solid in seconds. The electricity buzzed then flitted away leaving only two lumpy, bumpy heads protruding from the huge frozen slab of chocolate slab. One was crying slightly, the other was crying a lot.

"Excuse me!" said a voice which was surprisingly deep for a ten year old. "I'm Hank J Twizzler and these are my colleagues Chu Chong, Eva Gabriella Chomp, Herbert Dibdab and Flip Wrigley. Would you mind if we had some quality time alone with Blowhole and Snot?"

Maciii and J.B. checked to see everyone agreed.

"Sure! Why not? We got a phone call to make anyway!"

The door to the Solidifier swung open as the candy barons climbed onto the slabbed chocolate and slammed it shut behind them.

As Maciii, J.B., Deek and Samantha walked away all they heard was,

"Herbert! Hank! I can explain everything! Eva! Flip! Chu! Flip – where are you thinking of poking that stick?? Aaaaaaaaaaaaaaaarrgggggggggggggggggggggggggggggghhh hhhhhhhh!!!!"

Chapter Fifteen
...AND FINALLY...

The slicing 'copter blades of the F13 Da Vinci K2 whirled and twirled as it sat on the roof of the Chocolate Taj Mahal which was now surrounded by flapping SCENE OF CRIME tape. A regiment of MI3(and a bit) agents had arrived in the last hour by trucks, vans and unmarked cars – Operation Clean-Up was under way. Agents were picking and poking through debris, taking finger and toe prints, plucking the tiniest of confectionery evidence and sealing it in MI3(and a bit) plastic bags. Sniffer dogs scoured the scene unearthing contraband chocolate and the agency's top-line computer-geeks were busy hacking away at Blowhole's laptops. Captain Smitherington was scurrying about pointing and huffing and writing down important things.

At the Solidifier a group of agents armed with hammers and chisels carefully chipped away at the frozen chocolate.

"Don't chip so close!" ordered Blowhole, forgetting he was in no position to.

"Well, I suppose congratulations are in order!" said the Colonel, turning her back on the busy scene and addressing Maciii, J.B., Samantha and Deek. "It seems you have brought Operation Blowhole to a perfect conclusion. Well done. Of course, you are now under strict conditions of the Official Secrets Act and nothing you have seen or heard here can be repeated anywhere else. Ever." She nailed them with one of her don't-mess-with-me-or-I'll-mess-with-you looks. "Do you understand?"

The quartet nodded their heads.

"Good - now the operation is over you are to return to your normal lives…"

"Normal lives?" interjected J.B. "Mega-downer!"

"You will go about your lives as if nothing ever happened!" ordered the Colonel.

As she spoke a group of agents trundled passed with the silent and sad looking Goldenbum.

"My baby!" squealed Blowhole from the Solidifier. "My poor, poor baby! Would you, please, chip in the other direction?"

Suddenly, simultaneously, the most brilliant of brilliant ideas plopped into the combined minds of Maciii, J.B., Deek and Samantha.

"Wait!" Maciii commanded the trundling agents.

"Whatever are you doing?" spluttered the Colonel. "Whatever are they doing?" she spluttered at a shrugging Smitherington.

Goldenbum trundled to a halt and the quartet elbowed aside the agents and like a well-rehearsed routine began uncoupling it. Maciii grabbed a nearby 13-amp electricity supply and within seconds Goldenbum was blinking and bleeping once more.

"Whatever are you doing?" shouted Blowhole. "Take your hands off my bum!"

Maciii turned to Samantha. "Phone!" and she eagerly handed it over. J.B. and Deek were sliding open the giant Chocolate door revealing a beautiful night sky crowned by an awesome white moon.

"I asked you whatever are they doing?" the Colonel spluttered some more to Smitherington.

"Whatever are you doing?" Smitherington asked Maciii as he plugged Samantha's phone into Goldenbum. Maciii tapped his nose. "You'll see!"

Smitherington tapped his own nose and returned to his boss. He was about to tap her nose by way of explanation but thought better of it.

"I think it's a secret, ma'am!" he tapped his nose again.

"What do you mean secret? WE make secrets not them…" But the rest of her rant was left dangling in the night air as Goldenbum purred and hummed louder than it had ever done before, then slowly started to tilt on its golden legs until its under-side was in direct line with the moon. Everyone in the Taj Mahal stopped and watched.

"Directing audio to every computer on the planet!"

announced Maciii, once more jabbing the keyboard, then held the plugged e-phone before the Colonel's bewildered face like he was serving her a drink.

"Perhaps you'd care to press play, ma'am?"

And she did, and there was suddenly a blinding flash and a piercing yellow laser beam of light shot from Goldenbum. A nanosecond later the scowling face of Blowhole appeared on the face of the moon sneering down on its inhabitants and his cackling voice crackled across every speaker on the planet.

"You cretinous bunch of snivelling doofuses! Now I can tell you everything. There is no such thing as Downloadable Chocolate! It's a scam, a wheeze, a figment of my staggeringly impressive imagination! I have convinced the entire planet of its existence!"

The room, the moon and the planet fell silent.

In the Taj Mahal the silence was broken by the sound of handcuffs clicking on the wrists of an unchipped Blowhole.

"The greatest scam in the history of confectionery!" he muttered as an agent started tugging him away. "I could have been a multi billionaire. Just you wait, I'll be back. Snot, tell them I'll be back!" And with those last words Blowhole was dragged into a waiting black van. Snot stopped momentarily to address the group.

"I doubt it!" he said and then he was tugged away too.

"Well, well, well!" said the Colonel, slowly stepping over to the group followed by a nodding Smitherington. "Perhaps I was wrong!" Smitherington shifted his nod to a shake then back again a little confused. The quartet waited for her next words.

"Perhaps the world of covert intelligence would be a lot poorer for your absence. Perhaps, and you can say no if you wish, perhaps you'd all care to form the Junior Branch of MI3(and a bit) - starting immediately?"

The quartet whooped and hi-twentied each other.

"I'll take that as a yes, then. Smitherington, find them another assignment!"

THE END

OTHER BOOKS BY IAN BILLINGS

SAM HAWKINS –
PIRATE DETECTIVE,
AND THE CUTGLASS CUTLASS!

Yo ho ho and a bottle of grog! All aboard the Naughty
Lass for a hilarious piratical tale! Washed up pirate,
Sam Hawkins, is about to put his boldness and brains
to new use - as a pirate detective.

His first case is that of the stolen Cutglass Cutlass.
With only a super-intelligent octopus, some nibbled
red herrings and a bunch of mysteriously tiny footsteps
as clues, it's a puzzle as zany as it is perilous!

AVAILABLE FROM CABOODLE BOOKS!

OTHER BOOKS BY IAN BILLINGS

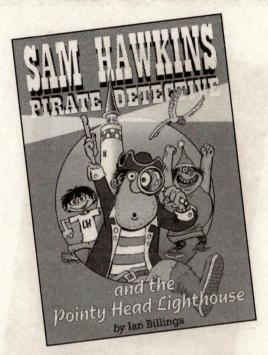

SAM HAWKINS AND THE POINTY HEAD LIGHTHOUSE

Sam Hawkins' wave of success following his discovery
of the Cutglass Cutlass has become more of a gentle
ripple on the low tide of Washed-upon-the Beach.

But just when it looks like Sam is going to have to
abandon ship there's a knock at the door - The Pointy
Head Lighthouse has been stolen!

AVAILABLE FROM CABOODLE BOOKS!

OTHER BOOKS

SPACE ROCKS!

Want a close encounter of the absurd kind or worse?
Then blast off with these aster-odes from across the looney verse!
Rockin' poems that are funny and ace!
I would tell you more, but there's not enough SPACE!!

AVAILABLE FROM CABOODLE BOOKS!